SKULL FLOWERS

JAZON DION FLETCHER

BACKWOODS PRESS

Dedicated to my family
Without their love and support
This book wouldn't exist
Thank you

CONTENTS

People are like skull flowers. Some need no help to grow upright and strong, others struggle, and need guidance along the way, some show promise, yet are lost amongst the weeds, while others perish, and never make it past the seed.

— THE PRIESTESS OF OBLIVION

PROLOGUE

Beyond the farthest star known to man, out amongst the darkness that knows no end, it is written in the Legends of the Old Wizard Bones that upon the completion of the Magnum Opus, the Great Architect of the Universe, an immortal androgyne of infinite cosmic power, crafted the Jewel of Wisdom with the aid of the ancient electronic arts. For he had learned to harness the power of the Prima Materia, the very essence of existence as it was then known. With the Jewel of Wisdom, he created the cosmos and placed it in a perfect order known as the Great Work of the Great Architect of the Universe.

The Great Architect of the Universe created the Heavenly Bodies known as the sun, the moon, the planets, and all of the stars in the sky. From these Heavenly Bodies, he gave life to the Flower Children in the Gardens of Eternity. Created they were in the likeness of his image. It was unto these Flower Children, because of their innocence, that the Great Architect of the Universe left the Jewel of Wisdom for safekeeping, for he knew they would not use it for evil. No unclean thought nor wicked thing dwelt amongst them. This act did not please those on the Divine Council of the Great Architect of the Universe, none more so than Oblivion, the Lord of the Void. It was Oblivion that murdered the Elder Gods, the Old Ones, that had existed since before the dawning of time, who in some tongues shall forever remain nameless. From them, he freed the Sintari, a race of humanoid-reptilian hybrids who could shape-shift and resemble whomever they so chose.

Oblivion longed to possess the Jewel of Wisdom for himself. It was at the time of its creation that, Mystre, his most loyal disciple, brought before him a servant girl named Psydonia, plucked from amongst one of his many faithful covens, that said unto him, "Allow me to put the petals of a skull flower into the cup of the Great Architect of the Universe while he feasts, so he will become intoxicated and sleep, that it might give you time to descend into the Gardens of Eternity and obtain the Jewel of Wisdom for thyself, so you may rise above the heavens, and become a Master of the Ancient Electronic Arts, for, upon that day, thou shalt become even greater than the Great Architect of the Universe, and have dominion over the whole of his creation, so that all therein, will worship you as a god."

The words of Psydonia pleased Oblivion, and so it was that Mystre took the petals from a skull flower, and the blood from a black widow spider, and did cast a spell over them so that Psydonia could place them in the chalice of the Great Architect of the Universe while he feasted. With each new sip of wine, the Great Architect of the Universe became more and more intoxicated until he excused himself from the presence of his Divine Council, and left for his chambers to slumber. As the Great Architect of the Universe fell to sleep, Oblivion and his disciples came before the Divine Council, and he said unto them, "If thou dost follow me into the Gardens of Eternity below to obtain the Jewel of Wisdom and swear upon your immortal souls an oath unto me, together, we will rise above the heavens and become even greater than the Great Architect of the Universe, for he keeps its secrets from us so that we shall remain in servitude."

The words of Oblivion tempted the Immortals of the Divine Council of the Great Architect of the Universe. The more they pondered upon his unholy lies, the more their immortal souls felt as though they were in bondage. Their spirits became destitute. So together, they descended from the heavens above, and down into the beautiful meadows of the Flower Children in the Gardens of Eternity below, where they sought after the Jewel of Wisdom until at long last they came upon it, and the Jewel of Wisdom was in the possession of Oblivion and his disciples.

The Flower Children were pure in spirit, peaceful, and their every way was untainted before Oblivion walked amongst them. They lived in harmony with the whole of the Great Architect's creation, in a feral, natural state, with the animals, the birds, and the plants around them. Civilization was unknown to them nor domestication. No fowl of the air, nor beast of the field, feared them. The whole of the Great Architect's creation was holy and precious in their eyes, even that which was covered by the sea. It was in their meadows, innocent to the plight and evils which would soon befall them, that Oblivion, with the aid of not only his disciples but the Sintari as well, therein did enslave the Flower Children. The Sintari forced them to build Oblivion a ziggurat, upon the top of which rested his temple, where from his throne, Oblivion would sit with the Jewel of Wisdom before him, and meditate upon all the secrets of the ancient electronic arts that the Great Architect of the Universe had hidden therein. All he learned was written in the Scrolls of Skeleton Bones by the Disciples of Oblivion, the most secret of that ancient wisdom being recorded in the Codex Magicka and guarded by Mystre.

Amongst the Immortals of the Divine Council of the Great Architect of the Universe, Oblivion divided the Gardens of Eternity and therein they took their pick of slaves from amongst the Flower Children. With the use of wicked and ancient forgotten sorceries and sciences, they divided the Flower Children from their natural state into man and woman and bred with them. The Immortals departed from Oblivion and from amongst their newly established kingdoms they did give unto him tithes and offerings of all they found in the lands bestowed unto them as he meditated both day and night in his temple upon that which the Jewel of Wisdom had revealed.

It was while Oblivion contemplated this most ancient wisdom that Mystre summoned Psydonia before his throne. In Oblivion's presence, she bowed before him, bathed in the light of the Jewel of Wisdom. After being baptized in the black waters pulled from the rivers that run through the Void, Mystre bestowed upon her the title of Priestess of Oblivion so that she could become his bride and share with him the gift of immortality. Their unholy union brought forth many offspring. But just as her beauty knew no end, neither did her cruelty, for unto an open lover's ear, she whispered unto Oblivion, "If thou dost exalt my beauty above all things and do love me, have those that once sat upon the Divine Council of the Great Architect of the Universe, that swore an eternal and unbreakable oath unto thee, have them cast forth their offspring into the fire from amongst those they have mingled their seed and demand that as part of their tithes and offerings that they must make burnt sacrifices unto idols that bare your image. Have them lift up thy name in praise while they kneel before you as the Emperor of the Universe, and the ruler of all things, both known and unknown."

The voice of Psydonia did soothe the wicked heart of Oblivion, and so it was commanded, that the Immortals of the Divine Council of the Great Architect of the Universe be forced to kneel before the Throne of Oblivion and worship him as the Emperor of the Universe. In screams of pain and demonic agony, the Disciples of Oblivion grabbed the offspring of the Flower Children and the Immortals of the Divine Council of the Great Architect of the Universe, one by one, and offered them up as burnt sacrifices unto idols baring the image of Oblivion and his lover, to celebrate their dominion over the Great Work of the Great Architect of the Universe. From those that did not flee from the wrath of Oblivion, they sacrificed all therein, except for those that the Immortals that once sat upon the Divine Council of the Great Architect of the Universe kept as wives, concubines, mistresses, and every type of perverted sex slave imaginable who found themselves defiled even amongst the Sintari. It was in these fires that Oblivion forged, the Midnight Sun, a sword as evil as the Void. In the pommel of the Midnight Sun, he placed the Jewel of Wisdom. This act filled the blade of the sword with the cosmic power to kill not only those that were immortal but even the Great Architect of the Universe who still lay sleeping, dreaming of that which only gods see when they slumber.

The cries of the Flower Children were not in vain, for they broke Mystre's spell over the Great Architect of the Universe, causing him to awaken from what felt like a sleep deeper than death itself. As their punishment, the Great Architect of the Universe stripped the

Immortals of his Divine Council of their immortality, and the temple the Flower Children were forced to build Oblivion, he destroyed as the two of them battled therein.

The fate of the Immortals was not to be Oblivion's, for he had become too powerful to strip of his immortality. The Great Architect of the Universe instead stripped Oblivion of his heavenly body, and of all of its magical power, then cast his spirit into the Void from whence he came. As he did so, the Midnight Sun fell from the hands of Oblivion to the floor of the temple, and the Jewel of Wisdom dislodged from the pommel of the sword. Psydonia fled in terror as the Great Architect of the Universe fixed his gaze upon her children and stripped them of their immortality and her of her eternal beauty but not her eternal life.

Alas, these acts caused even more sorrow for the Flower Children who did not mingle their seed with the Immortals of the Divine Council of the Great Architect of the Universe. In the beautiful meadows surrounding the Gardens of Eternity, as the Spirit of Oblivion was cast into the Void and departed from its heavenly body, and the beauty of Psydonia withered and began to fade, the Great Architect of the Universe wept for the Flower Children when he saw what the wickedness of Oblivion had done as his spirit tried in futility to bind itself to the whole of the Great Architect's creation, and how in that final act, the Gardens of Eternity were given over to ruin and decay. It was while the Flower Children wept and they fled into the wastelands of the Golden Triangle, far away from the Immortal Kingdoms, that the Great Architect of the Universe felt a pain upon his side and saw that the blade of the Midnight Sun had pierced his flesh and poisoned him with the unholy magic that Oblivion had invoked therein. It seemed that while they battled in his temple for the fate of the cosmos, Oblivion had succeeded in delivering upon his former master, a fatal wound, that would soon cause the breath of life to be taken from the body of Great Architect of the Universe and given up to the Four Winds of the Gardens of Eternity, for therein would the descendants of the Flower Children and the Immortals that once sat upon his Divine Council dig their shallow graves until they were no more. As he fell to his knees, upon the floor of the Temple of Oblivion, the Great Architect of the Universe engraved his sigil, so that Oblivion could not easily escape from the Void, and would be sealed therein. It was only once the Sigil of the Great Architect of the Universe was complete that he ascended into the heavens and hid himself in an unmapped region of the cosmos as the whole of his creation became a funeral pyre.

It is with this in mind that we begin our story...

1

DON'T BREAK THE OATH

The Imperial City of Zohar was a dying whore. A sprawling city-state swallowing up all of the former pastoral lands of what remained of the Gardens of Eternity not divided up amongst the Immortal Kingdoms. She was an industrial wasteland, amidst a rotting bayou, that stretched itself out for as far as the eye could see, whose streets moaned with the pleasures of her orgasmic blasphemies. Tryptamine crystals powered it all.

Many of the descendants of the Flower Children sought refuge within the capital of the Black Sun Empire and were in search of fresh food, clean water, shelter, and healing. The bones of the dead paved the roads so that the Think Tanks of the Imperial Armada could roll across the land unopposed. Engraved on the side of each Think Tank was the Sigil of Oblivion, an inverted five-pointed star, inside of a circle, at the center of which was the face of a black mutant goat with only one giant eye in the center of its forehead. The orders of their futile peacekeeping mission in the Golden Triangle were to seize the tryptamine mines the Orphans of Doom used to create the mutagen Nekrotek.

In great pain and sorrow, the descendants of the Flower Children brought their women, their children, the sick, and the dead wrapped in burial cloth in the hopes that they might find some respite from their woe. There were boils, infections, and pustulations amongst them. Some even had maggotoids crawling underneath their skin. Nekrosis ran rampant. Unbeknownst to them all, the resurrection of Oblivion was at hand. Many faithful believers wailed before the ancient walls of the ziggurat their ancestors had built. The Occult Bureau's cybernetic drones guarded it day and night. Unmanned Scavenger UAV's patrolled the sky overhead like vultures waiting for the descendants of the Flower Children to die so that they could feast upon their remains.

Centuries had passed since the Great Architect of the Universe cast Oblivion into the Void. In that time, the Immortal Kings, those that once sat upon the Divine Council of the Great Architect of the Universe, passed away and many of their names became forgotten by the descendants of the Flower Children and the descendants of the offspring of Oblivion and Psydonia. The Legends of the Old Wizard Bones shared a similar fate in many of their minds. Here in this land their heirs came together and united their kingdoms into an empire that now reigned over every square inch of the Great Architect's most beloved creation and all that dwelt within it.

Mystre, known to the descendants of the Flowers Children as the Hierophant of the cults of the Priestess of Oblivion, chanted his prayers outside of the entrance to the rebuilt Temple of Oblivion. Upon the Altar of the Sleeping Virgin, the Disciples of Oblivion placed one of the temple's prostitutes. Mystre cut the throat of the woman with a sacred dagger. Her blood spewed everywhere as the Gateway to the Void slowly rose along the horizon and the sun set as though it were dying in the last breath of a temple prostitute's kiss.

"Bring our cause before the Most High!" cried the descendants of the Flower Children, yet their suffering would fall upon deaf ears, for Mystre cared for no one, least of all the sick and the dead. Centurions in the Order of the Trapezoid stood before them just outside the trenchworks of the old ruins that surrounded the ziggurat. Each centurion held a Widowmaker, a scythe-like weapon with a laser for a blade. Many teeming with disease coughed and spread the scourge of nekrosis as one amongst the centurions said, "The Supreme Council of the Black Sun Empire has decreed that all except authorized personnel are forbidden to enter upon the grounds of the ziggurat or anywhere amongst its ancient ruins!"

Above the entrance to the temple's innermost sanctum were engraved the words, DON'T BREAK THE OATH. Inside, gathered before the Jewel of Wisdom, sat the members of the Supreme Council of the Black Sun Empire. It was here, amongst the many relics of the old religion, that Governor Champagne, the Exchequer of the Board of Governors of the Imperial Central Bank of the Black Sun Empire, was hopelessly pleading his case. He believed he was right in refusing to fund a new and dangerous experimental nekrobiotic and that it should not be administered to the inhabitants of the city without proper oversight and testing beforehand. It was a plea that before he ever entered the temple, he knew would be a waste of breath.

"The peacekeeping mission that this empire has raged in the Golden Triangle has cost us more lives and treasure than any of us could have possibly imagined and for what? Does anyone here even remember?" said Governor Champagne. He held up a copy of Zohar's largest newspaper, *The Imperial Times*. On the front cover, above the fold, was a picture of one of the tryptamine mines occupied by the Orphans of Doom. It was in flames after an attack on it by General Grindcore and the Imperial Armada.

The headline read, WRECKERS OF CIVILIZATION.

"I'll take care in reminding you," continued Governor Champagne. "The Orphans of Doom were labeled a terrorist organization by the House of the Black Widow, upon the instruction of this very body. They did so after confirmation from the Occult Bureau that they had seized an illegal shipment of an extremely lethal weapon known as Nekrotek in our city. A mutagenic made from the toxic byproducts of the tryptamine crystals mined and refined in the Golden Triangle. The knowledge that such a sinister and diabolical weapon had been altered to be even more deadly when carried in the belly of a lethal cybernetic organism known as a Nekrobyte disturbed many. When the news that these Nekrobytes were being unleashed upon the inhabitants of the Golden Triangle if they did not co-operate with the Orphans of Doom, not only did this news enrage our people, but it shook them to their very core when those diseased with nekrosis began to flood across the border of the empire and into Zohar. The fear that the Orphans of Doom would unleash such a weapon in the capital was real and that there would be little hope of survival for our way of life if it came true.

"In response to their cries, the House of the Black Widow voted unanimously to close all imperial points of entry along our border with the Golden Triangle. This council ratified the House of the Black Widow's vote and ordered the Imperial Armada, under the command of General Grindcore, to put an end to the terrorist activity of the Orphans of Doom once and for all.

"Controlled Substances Incorporated recommended that we inoculate our people along with the refugees fleeing the carnage in the Golden Triangle. The nekrobiotic they proposed for such a task, known as Nekron, is an untested and possibly toxic experimental miracle drug that we were all promised would save our people if they found themselves exposed to a terrorist attack that contained any form of Nekrotek or Nekrobyte currently sold openly and mind you, illegally, on the Dark Web's many clandestine marketplaces. This proposal did not sit well with our people. It is well documented and not some fanciful conspiracy theory that the IPTV news reports refused to admit that many of the refugees began to riot upon hearing that they were to take part in an experimental and quite possibly lethal inoculation program.

"To make these matters even worse than what they already are, Chancellor Thorn, seemingly ignorant of the current discontent on the streets of the capital, now foolishly proposes, that I fund and support Supreme Council Resolution 33. Those of us who have read this resolution find themselves sworn to secrecy under the threat of imprisonment and death. Supreme Council Resolution 33 requires only one thing of me that I fund the forced administration of Controlled Substances Incorporated's nekrobiotic. And who will enforce this resolution? The Occult Bureau and the Imperial Armada, in a joint task force operation, under the command of General Grindcore, whose mission will be to patrol the streets of Zohar, together, to ensure that the inhabitants of the capital comply with this council's demands regardless of their legal status as citizens."

"The people overwhelmingly voted for me in the last election or do I have to remind you of that?" interrupted Xavier Thorn as he rose to defend himself. Xavier was the leader of the Brimstone Society, the House of the Black Widow's majority party, and also chancellor of said house. "They knew my platform."

"An election tainted with allegations of fraud!" shouted Governor Champagne.

"You're beginning to sound like an oath breaker, Champagne," said Xavier.

"There should be no doubt about my loyalty in this temple!" shouted Governor Champagne.

"No one here is questioning your loyalty amongst us," said Xavier, "but I am forced to digress when I remind this body that the intelligence reports provided by the Occult Bureau were the reason General Grindcore and the Imperial Armada were allowed to patrol the streets of Zohar in the first place. These reports provided to not only Governor Champagne but to every member of the House of the Black Widow, on both sides of the aisle, outlined the obvious threats to our city. I emphasize that everyone within both parties, every member of the Checkmate Club, and every member of the Brimstone Society, received copies of these classified documents. It is no secret that every single solitary member of the board of governors at the Imperial Central Bank, except for Governor Champagne, voted to release the funds. The Imperial Armada must be allowed to patrol the streets of Zohar and oversee the administration of Controlled Substances Incorporated's nekrobiotic to all of its inhabitants. It was known then, as it is known now, that not every single terrorist member of the Orphans of Doom was rounded up in the Armada's raids on their tryptamine mines. I have spoken personally with General Grindcore and with Special Agent Scarzensky, the Occult Bureau's lead investigator into the whereabouts of Viirus, the leader of the Orphans of Doom. Both of them have told me, that without a shadow of a doubt, those who escaped the raids in the Golden Triangle are now operating sleeper cells throughout the city, under his command. If anything, we should be thanking General Grindcore, the Occult Bureau, and Controlled Substances Incorporated for what they have done, not only for this city but the empire as a whole."

"A company in which you have a vested interest I might add," said Governor Champagne.

"My investments and involvement with the board of directors of Controlled Substances Incorporated are perfectly legal and well within the guidelines established by the House of the Black Widow," said Xavier.

"Of course," Governor Champagne sarcastically remarked.

"Must I remind this body that as volunteers, both Governor Champagne and his daughter were inoculated with the nekrobiotic in question to ease the fears of the refugee population and that the two of them are still in perfect health to this very day?" said Xavier.

"My daughter suffered a miscarriage that almost cost her, her life, because of that accursed nekrobiotic and you know it!" shouted Governor Champagne.

A spirit of discontentment filled the room.

"Indeed, it is tragic that your daughter lost her beloved child," said Councilman Soros, "but there is no proof that it was the nekrobiotic in question that caused her body to abort the fetus. Was it not, in fact, several days later when she did, so sorrowfully, lose said child?"

Xavier remained silent while Governor Champagne answered Councilman Soros' question.

"You are correct," he said.

"Correct in which part," said Councilman Soros, "that there is no proof linking her misfortune to the nekrobiotic in question, or that she lost said child several days after the administration of said nekrobiotic?"

"You are correct in your statement that it was several days after she received the nekrobiotic in question that she miscarried her child," said Governor Champagne. "However, the reason that there is no proof linking the nekrobiotic to her miscarriage is because this council voted to have her medical records seized. How was our family supposed to conduct an investigation without those records?"

"This council examined the records in question, and it was our ruling, based upon the sound judgment at the time, that there was no link between the two events, and that the medical records of your daughter should remain sealed because their contents could pose a threat to imperial security and violate the empire's trade secrets agreement with Controlled Substances Incorporated," said Councilman Soros. "Your mind, however, seems to have become clouded. Why is it that you cannot accept our ruling Governor Champagne? What is it as of late that has caused you to not only become combative with the chancellor of the House of the Black Widow but with our council as well? Without an excuse worthy of being bellowed back and forth between the Four Winds, I see no reason for the Imperial Central Bank not to fund the nekrobiotic administration program of Controlled Substances Incorporated."

"Nor, do I," seconded Xavier. "The board of governors has spoken. What could you possibly have to say in your defense that would be a good enough excuse to continue to block this medical breakthrough that the citizens of our empire so desperately need at this troubled time?"

Governor Champagne stood silent for a moment.

"It is my belief," he said, "that someone, who knows, perhaps even the chancellor himself, wished me dead because of my refusal to accept the Emissions Guild's decision to recommend that the Occult Bureau drop their investigation into the nekrotik pollution coming from Industrial Plant No. 213 owned by Controlled Substances Incorporated, and that the lethal nekrobiotic that almost killed my daughter was intended for me."

"Another outlandish conspiracy theory," said Xavier, "based on what evidence, your broken heart?"

"These are serious allegations Governor Champagne that borderline on delusional," said Councilman Soros. "Our ruling was that there was no link between your daughter's medical problems and the nekrobiotic manufactured by Controlled Substances Incorporated, yet here you stand, ready to make an allegation against the legally elected chancellor of the House of the Black Widow without so much as one shred of proof. Have you lost your mind, man?"

"No," said Governor Champagne. "I have not."

The Supreme Council of the Black Sun Empire had heard enough.

"It seems," said Councilman Soros, without a single moment of hesitation in his voice, "that what has been presented to us here today is an example of why it might be in the best interest of this council to vote on the real issue at hand. Should we remove Governor Champagne from his post at the Imperial Central Bank because of his refusal to accept the judgment of this council? It is my recommendation that we do so and that we disband the House of the

Black Widow until a new election can be held to replace those within it that might share Governor Champagne's views."

"I concur with Councilman Soros," said Councilman Boule. "Such behavior in these times is an act of treason and should be punished right alongside any act of terrorism the Orphans of Doom have committed in the Golden Triangle."

"I'm inclined to agree as well," said Councilman Ulrich.

"So say we all," said Councilman Giger.

The remaining councilmen and councilwomen nodded in agreement.

Sitting on the Throne of Oblivion, atop a dais in the middle of the Supreme Council, with the Midnight Sun in a sword pedestal to her left and a robotic black panther named Maximillion sitting to her right, Destiny Giavasis, Princess of Zohar, had heard enough.

"Perhaps these matters would be better discussed another day?" she said. "Let us rejoice for the Day of the Lord is upon us. There is a gala underway at the Crystal Ball during this Festival of the Dead to help raise money for the sick and the homeless that have poured as of late into the capital, and I'm sure it would please our people to see us in good cheer."

Princess Destiny's words moved Governor Champagne.

"It was not my intention to ruin the festive atmosphere of our fair city this day," he said.

"Nor, was it mine," said Xavier.

Princess Destiny placed her hand atop the head of Maximillion.

"Of one mind and in one accord, allow yourselves, if only for a brief moment, to put your differences to rest for today," she said. "Rejoice, for there is much to celebrate. After so many centuries the Temple of Oblivion is finally rebuilt, and soon, this terrorist threat that has plagued us for so long shall too come to an end."

2

APARTMENT 147

In Apartment 147 of the Ivory Towers, Alexis Champagne, the only daughter of Governor Champagne, was seated at her boudoir. She was an iconic beauty. In the mirror, Alexis admired an extravagant necklace made of diamonds, accentuated with a heart-shaped locket that lay around her neck. She made sure it didn't cover her new butterfly tattoo. Alexis sat down a glass of wine next to a tray of exotic apples, caramels, and cheeses, for like her namesake, she was given over to much drink, but not so much as to be unladylike. From a bottle labeled *Love Potion No. 69* she sprayed a little perfume on herself while the diamonds from her XOXO watch (pronounced Zoh-Zoh) sparkled on her wrist.

808 (pronounced Eight-oh-Eight) sat on the floor with his legs crossed. He was playing a game of Robot Football 2099. 808 loved the game and planned to compete in the Cyborg Bowl held at Abracadabra's Arcade at the first of the new year. His jet black armor reflected every play as he made his way down the field. Yard after yard he struggled to inch himself closer to the goal line. 808 just couldn't seem to get his ground game going. The NPC defensive team was stone-walling his running back. 808 opened his playbook. He selected a shotgun formation. 808 hiked the ball. The offensive line held the defensive line back. All three of 808's wide receivers ran deep downfield. One of the defensive linemen broke through the

offensive line as a wide receiver ran it into the end zone. 808 fired the ball from his quarterback's arm cannon. Suddenly, the wide receiver had two men on him. An interception looked inevitable. Everything moved in slow motion. 808's receiver jumped and caught the ball.

"Touchdown!" yelled the announcer.

Alexis got up from her boudoir and picked up a keychain in the shape of a heart-shaped hologram from off of her nightstand.

"Don't forget your Grimoire," she said. 808 pulled the Headbanger Headphones off of his head, jumped up off the floor, grabbed his Grimoire off of the top of his backpack sitting on the kitchen table, and ran in behind Alexis.

"Goodbye, 808," said the voice of the television. A Maestro OS logo appeared on its screen. The television powered down and went to sleep.

808 closed the front door of the apartment behind them.

In the parking garage of the Ivory Towers sat Alexis' sports car, the Shadow Runner. The Shadow Runner was an experimental patrol car designed by Professor Proxy. It was the first of its kind. The car's paint job was jet black. The hood ornament was a heart-shaped hologram just like her keychain. It shimmered and sparkled like it was made of diamonds when Alexis remotely powered on the electrical system.

"D'jew you bring some music?" said Alexis.

808 nodded his head, yes. The door to the Shadow Runner opened. There was a heads-up display on the windshield of the Shadow Runner that synced with the contact lenses Alexis was wearing. 808 clicked the E.S.P. button on his Grimoire. E.S.P. stood for Electronic, Sync, Protocol. The button synced the screen of 808's Grimoire with the touchscreen in the dash and allowed him to control the Shadow Runner's electronic devices from his tablet. 808 tuned the radio to Hot2Trot.fm

Alexis gripped the steering wheel like she was about to play a video game. She stomped the power pedal to the floor. Flames poured out of the exhaust pipes. The Shadow Runner raced out of the parking garage, into the street, and onto the on-ramp of the Super Highway.

Vrooooom!

The Shadow Runner passed by two armored patrol cars driven by

Enforcer Drones that were sitting in the median of the Super Highway. On the side of each of the patrol cars was written the acronym S.T.A.L.K.E.R.

S.T.A.L.K.E.R. stood for Strategic, Tactical, Armored, K-9, Enforcement, Robot. They had a two-way communications link with the H.I.V.E.

H.I.V.E. stood for Humanoid, Information, Virtualization, Extranet. It was a centralized supercomputing network designed by Dr. Necropolis that connected and controlled all of the drones, regardless of their type, throughout the capital city of Zohar. The Hive was stored deep in the bowels of the ziggurat in the central command center of the Occult Bureau.

In the distance, Alexis could see a billboard streaming a WXTZ Channel 13 news broadcast about the continuing riots in the refugee camps. Many parts of Zohar had become no-go zones because of the crime. Reports of rape ran rampant. Murder seemed to be in vogue. There were reports that the Orphans of Doom hid amongst the refugees. Outside of his front passenger side window, 808 could see the Ferris wheel at the Laissez Fair on the Crystal Ball's fairgrounds come into view. A beautiful fireworks display exploded in the night sky revealing the Star Gazer, one of the Occult Bureau's many aerial ships that scanned the city for unauthorized activity.

The Shadow Runner exited the Super Highway underneath a sign labeled, *Crystal Ball*. Alexis merged in line with the traffic in front of her. The Shadow Runner came to rest in front of a checkpoint manned by some mercenaries in the Imperial Armada. Alexis was waved on through once the Shadow Runner was inspected, and one of the Occult Bureau's security details scanned its license plate. A Security Drone directed the car into the valet in front of the Crystal Ball where Officer Whistle Britches, one of her father's loyal friends, was blowing his police whistle. The moment he spotted the Shadow Runner, he ran toward the car and helped Alexis with her door.

"Well, aren't you the belle of the ball," flirted a tad bit tubby Officer Whistle Britches.

Alexis appreciated the compliment.

"Thank you, Whistle Britches," she replied. "I see you're as handsome as ever. If I didn't have 808 here with me, I do believe I'm tempted enough to make you my date for this evening."

"Well, I do what I can," said Officer Whistle Britches. As he blushed, a limousine pulled up to the curb chauffeured by Special Agent Scarzensky. He was as grotesque and as hideous as a rotting stump full of dead spiders. "Excuse me," grunted Officer Whistle Britches when he saw the limousine. He staggered off all bumble-footed with two toots and a happy poot.

Inside of the limousine, Xavier was speaking with Councilman Soros via a secure communications link within the limousine's entertainment system.

"If Governor Champagne does not come to his senses I want him silenced," said Councilman Soros. His image streamed on the screen in front of Xavier. *"Do we understand one another?"*

"I doubt anything I say will change his mind," said Xavier.

"Then have Special Agent Scarzensky kill him," said Councilman Soros. *"I've heard enough about his daughter's medical troubles to last me a lifetime."*

"As you wish," said Xavier.

Councilman Soros ended the transmission.

Through his window, Xavier could see Alexis and 808. They were walking up the red carpet and toward the entrance of the Crystal Ball. A slight wind gust blew up the dress of Alexis almost revealing her panties.

"Alexis look this way!" shouted the Glitterati. The lights from their cameras flashed over and over again. For a second, Officer Whistle Britches went blind from all the flashing lights. He stumbled and tried to regain his composure. Special Agent Scarzensky swung open the driver's side door of the limo from the inside. The impact from the door knocked Officer Whistle Britches to the ground.

"Uuuuggghhh!" he moaned.

Special Agent Scarzensky stepped out of the limousine. Officer Whistle Britches struggled to scramble away on his hands and knees. Special Agent Scarzensky kicked Officer Whistle Britches in the butt and shouted, "Get out of the way you twit!"

3

SKYBOX

While Officer Whistle Britches struggled to his feet, inside the Crystal Ball, Alexis and 808 made their way to the Skybox where Governor Champagne was not only entertaining Princess Destiny, but, the board members on the board of directors of Controlled Substances Incorporated, his fellow governors on the board of governors at the Imperial Central Bank, and the elected officials on the Emissions Guild. Carlyle Manzini, the CEO of Controlled Substances Incorporated, was in attendance as well.

"The only way your nekrobiotic will receive funding from the Imperial Central Bank is if I am allowed to form an oversight committee therein with myself serving as its chairman to look into the matters that now concern our citizenry," said Governor Champagne. "Before the House of the Black Widow even considers whether it will vote to allow the distribution of the current line of nekrobiotics the public must know the results of my committee's investigation into the safety of your nekrobiotic."

"Whatever you need to put your concern with our nekrobiotic to rest," said Manzini, "I am more than happy to provide."

"So then we are in agreement that you will support the creation of such a committee and co-operate with its investigation?" said Governor Champagne.

"I will," said Manzini.

Alexis entered the Skybox with 808. Governor Champagne was none-to-pleased to see her choice of evening attire, nor the new butterfly tattoo on the back of her neck. He didn't have any problem with letting her know it either.

"Where did you get that outfit?" said Governor Champagne.

"You don't like it?" said Alexis.

"Your mother would roll over in her grave if she saw you in such a dress," said Governor Champagne. "And that tattoo on your neck!"

"Father, you're embarrassing me," said Alexis.

"I don't know how you're practically naked!" said Governor Champagne.

"I think she looks exquisite," said Manzini.

"You would," said Governor Champagne. He noticed 808 playing a game of *Pentagrams* on his Grimoire by the side of Alexis. "And, what is this?"

"This is 808, he's the project I've been working on with Professor Proxy," said Alexis. It was under Professor Proxy's watchful eye and tutelage that she'd earned her Ph.D. in Cybernetic Biology.

"Well, it's good to see he's doing something worthwhile with his endowment," said Governor Champagne.

"She's a grown woman you old coot! Let her have some fun!" said Princess Destiny. She slapped Governor Champagne upside the head with the evening's scheduled program of events and said to Alexis, "You look lovely my dear."

"Thank you," said Alexis. "Father is always pestering me about my choice in clothes or not living up to his expectations of me."

"Might I inquire to whom you're wearing?" said Princess Destiny.

"It's part of the Lonely Souls Collection," said Alexis.

"I look forward to seeing their new line unveiled this evening," said Princess Destiny.

"As do I," said Alexis.

"We all look forward to the vast array of exotic garments soon to be laid out before our eyes," said Governor Champagne. "However, it does not change the simple fact of life that the IPTV networks have started to refer to you as Bubbles because of your childish behavior. You should do your part, like our ancestors before you, and not shirk your duties to the royal family of Zohar, young lady. You should be by the side of Princess Destiny so that she will always have someone there whom she can trust and confide in, that she knows, without the shadow of a doubt, has the best interest of our people in their heart. You're unique amongst our people my dear sweet child. You are of the bloodlines of descendants of the Flower Children and the offspring of Oblivion and Psydonia. The dedication of your life to bringing unity to the peoples of this world so that one day they might stand hand in hand with love in their hearts for one another like your mother and I once did, must always be your number one priority. It is why I have always encouraged you in your cadet training and why I hound you to achieve your highest potential when it concerns your education. Our people need good women like yourself in these troubled times, now more than ever."

"The way father talks, you'd think I didn't know how to properly handle a Widowmaker," joked Alexis.

Princess Destiny, a dainty beauty herself, giggled. She enjoyed Alexis' company.

"Carlyle was just telling me about the cryotherapy he underwent to remove some liver spots on his hands," said Princess Destiny. "I tell you his hands look younger than mine."

"Is that so?" said Alexis. "Perhaps I should look into this treatment for myself. Mine always seem to stay so dry and cracked. I fear that they might appear to have once belonged to an old crone."

"It was a simple procedure," said Manzini. "Nothing as cutting edge as the robot you brought with you this evening."

Jeeves, the personal butler of Governor Champagne, approached 808. He could see that 808 might have a hard time seeing the fashion show from his seat, being that he was half the size of everyone around him.

"Would you care for a high chair, sir?" Jeeves asked 808. 808 raised his middle finger. Jeeves cocked one eye and glared at 808 like he'd spotted a spoiled brat. "I'll take that as a no."

Princess Destiny, on the other hand, was fascinated with 808.

"Does he eat?" she said.

"He likes sushi, but he mostly lives off of gothsicles and energy drinks," said Alexis.

"Sounds more like the kids in the arcade than a robot," said Xavier with a sheepish grin on his face and Special Agent Scarzensky by his side.

"Chancellor Thorn," said Governor Champagne acknowledging Xavier's presence begrudgingly.

Alexis' stomach began to turn.

"Father, if you'll excuse me," she coldly hissed in Xavier's direction.

Princess Destiny hated to see her leave.

"It's been a pleasure talking to you," she said.

"And, you as well," said Alexis. She grabbed 808 by the hand and hurried out of the Skybox. A robotic cockroach ran out from underneath Special Agent Scarzensky's pants leg and scurried along on the floor behind them.

Xavier wasted no time in getting on Governor Champagne's nerves.

"Perhaps it would be wise if we took this time to discuss more delicate matters?" he said.

"You're beating a dead horse, Thorn," said Governor Champagne. "I've already discussed the particulars with Manzini. We've agreed to the formation of an oversight committee at the Imperial Central Bank with myself serving as its chairman. Before the House of the Black Widow even considers whether it will vote to allow the distribution of the current line of nekrobiotics the public will know the results of my committee's investigation into their safety."

"There's no need to go to all that trouble when you could just have the funds released by the Imperial Central Bank this evening," said Xavier. "You have the power, you and you alone, to fund this nekrobiotic and its distribution. Allow the Checkmate Club and the Brimstone Society to come together in a bipartisan fashion before something terrible happens. Be the leader that proves once and for all to our people that there is not one nay vote amongst us that has a question as to the safety of Controlled Substances Incorporated's nekrobiotic."

"It would make this festive occasion even more enjoyable for the people, who have already made so many donations, to hear what Chancellor Thorn suggests," said Manzini. He seemed more than ready to back out of the deal he'd just made with Governor Champagne.

"I invited the entire board of directors of Controlled Substances Incorporated to the gala this evening for this very purpose," said Xavier. "Together with Princess Destiny let's speak to the sick and the dying that are flooding into our city and give them hope. Wouldn't that be wonderful, Your Highness?"

"It would," said Princess Destiny. "There's no need to anger Councilman Soros or the Supreme Council any further. I agree with Chancellor Thorn that at this time in our empire's history, the Nekron he wishes to distribute would be a blessing to our people."

"You see even our beloved princess agrees with me. Release the funds and speak to those in the House of the Black Widow that look to you for guidance," said Xavier. "Show them that you are a statesman whose leadership is one, not of a rabble-rouser, but of a peacemaker. Do this for us all so that we may steer clear of the wrath of Councilman Soros and the Supreme Council, least they have the House of the Black Widow disbanded."

Governor Champagne didn't care what Xavier said. Deep down in his heart, he knew that Xavier was up to no good and that to cast his lot in with him would be to cast his lot in with a servant of Oblivion.

"The only way that will ever happen is over my dead body," said Governor Champagne.

You could see it written all over the face of Xavier. He was sick and tired of trying to convince Governor Champagne to change his mind.

"It grieves me to hear that, my dear governor," said Xavier. "Really, it does."

The fact Xavier wouldn't shut up, and the thought of what the nekrobiotic had already done to Alexis filled Governor Champagne with a white-hot rage. He could stand his presence no longer.

"Our business is done here, sir!" shouted Governor Champagne at the top of his lungs to the astonishment of Xavier.

The Skybox became as quiet as a grave.

"I'm sorry to have wasted your time," said Xavier. He turned and slithered toward the exit of the Skybox like a slug with Special Agent Scarzensky in tow. Jeeves held the door open for them like he was waiting for someone to come around and pick up the trash. Xavier and

Special Agent Scarzensky stepped into the foyer together. A stench of agony and despair was in the air. Embarrassment was not something Xavier handled well. To be screamed at like a dog in such a public setting was more than he could bear.

Jeeves shut the door to the Skybox behind them.

Special Agent Scarzensky pressed the down button on the wall.

"You know what to do," said Xavier.

Special Agent Scarzensky nodded that he understood to the sound of the elevator door opening.

Tiiing!

4

PODCASTER

Outside of the Crystal Ball, all of the gala's guests were now inside except for a few cameramen loading up their gear into a WXTZ Channel 13 news van. In the distance, the Ferris wheel of the Laissez Fair continued to spin. All appeared peaceful. A mercenary in the Imperial Armada lit up a cigarette atop his Imperial Think Tank. Officer Whistle Britches was in a tiny patrol car known as a Podcaster. It looked like a jellybean on four wheels powered by a few photon cells the size of a lunch box. The mercenary shook his head in disbelief when Officer Whistle Britches passed by. In the passenger seat of the Podcaster beside Officer Whistle Britches was his loyal guard dog and best friend, Floppy.

"*Rarf! Rarf!*" barked Floppy with his paws against the window when he saw the mercenary.

"Floppy, sit down!" shouted Officer Whistle Britches. Floppy didn't listen. Instead, he jumped in Officer Whistle Britches lap and licked him in the face. "That's a good boy. Yes, he is. That's ah my buddy," said Officer Whistle Britches to Floppy. As Floppy showered Officer Whistle Britches with affection, his mood began to change. Nothing looked out of the ordinary when Floppy sat down. Officer Whistle Britches turned the wheel of the Podcaster and entered the staging area behind the Crystal Ball. It was at that moment that the Podcaster and all inside found themselves blocked by several Imperial Personnel Transports. A swarm of the Occult Bureau's Tactical Drones poured out of the back of them and assembled into formation in front of Special Agent Scarzensky. At first Officer Whistle Britches thought it must be just some type of drill, that was until he saw, Viirus, the leader of the Orphans of Doom, as he stepped out of the back of one of the Imperial Personnel Transports.

Officer Whistle Britches slammed on the Podcaster's brakes. The tires of the Podcaster came to a screeching halt. The Tactical Drones, all at the same time, looked in the direction of Officer Whistle Britches.

"Get him!" screamed Special Agent Scarzensky.

Two Battle Androids approached the Podcaster. Officer Whistle Britches powered the Podcaster into reverse and spun the car around. Battle Android DRN-1, codenamed, Assault, and Battle Android DRN-2, codenamed, Battery both locked and loaded two Metalstorm sub-machine guns. When they opened fire, the back windshield of the Podcaster shattered. Glass flew everywhere. Battle Android DRN-2, codenamed, Battery, threw a small defragmentation grenade at the Podcaster. It exploded and sent a distortion field rippling through the loading dock. The distortion field ended just behind the Podcaster in a static cloud of kinetic energy that sent the disabled Podcaster flying end over end into a deep drainage ditch behind the Crystal Ball. When it hit the bottom of the ditch, there was a huge explosion.

Back in the Skybox, all seemed well. The board members on the board of directors of Controlled Substances Incorporated, the governors on the board of governors at the Imperial Central Bank and the elected officials on the Emissions Guild were gone. Many of them now sat drunk next to the runway. The rest were putting stardust up their noses with the models backstage.

The smartphone in the Manzini's pocket vibrated. He slid it out. The text message on the screen read, *322*

The Orphans of Doom, guided by Viirus, had already begun to enter into the Crystal Ball from the staging area outside and disarm what little security stood between them and the Pelican Ballroom where the evening's fashion show was scheduled to take place. One of Viirus' many orphans hit the up button on the first elevator that crossed their path. When the doors opened, the orphan stepped inside and armed the suicide vest he was wearing.

"Excuse me," said Manzini. "Nature calls."

Governor Champagne waved off Manzini. He paid him no mind whatsoever. Manzini passed by Princess Destiny. She was henpecking Governor Champagne about his altercation with Xavier.

"Perhaps you should hear him out," said Princess Destiny. "He seemed to be sincere."

Governor Champagne couldn't believe Princess Destiny was so naive as to believe Xavier could be trusted.

"The man tried to murder me," he said. "That is something I will not soon forget. I wouldn't be surprised if he tried to kill you next or put that ghoulish thing following him around up to doing it."

"Governor Champagne, really!" said Princess Destiny with a look of utter astonishment on her face. "You can't possibly still believe that Xavier tried to murder you, much less that he is now in the process of hatching some plot against me?"

"Do not be so foolish as to underestimate Xavier," said Governor Champagne. "Blind yourself to his machinations, and you might be a princess today, but tomorrow, well, you could easily find yourself with your throat cut before the Throne of Oblivion."

"If you keep talking like this, the Supreme Council will have you arrested," said Princess Destiny. "Councilman Soros approached me after the council adjourned and he tried to convince me that it was in the empire's best interest that we have you committed to an insane asylum."

Governor Champagne was unfazed by the news.

"I have no doubt that he wishes me gone," he said. "His push for a vote to have me removed from the Imperial Central Bank is ample evidence of that. But it does not change the fact that what I have said to you this evening is the truth. Do not ever say that I did not warn you."

Princess Destiny would hear none of it.

"Voting for your removal from the Imperial Central Bank and plotting to murder you are two separate things," she said. "You're being paranoid."

"I am not paranoid," said Governor Champagne.

"All that I'm saying is that if you don't want to find yourself removed from your post at the Imperial Central Bank, you need to choose your words more carefully in your dealings with Councilman Soros," said Princess Destiny. "And when it comes to Xavier, you need to be more open to what the man has to say. Instead of dwelling on the hatred you now have for him, perhaps it would be wise if you instead dwelt on the happier times that your houses shared?"

"Manzini's trouble with the Emissions Guild was the beginning of the strife between us," said Governor Champagne. "Xavier knows this. I never quarreled with his father when he was chancellor nor did I wake up one morning out of boredom and wish to see my family destroyed. When Alexis accepted his marriage proposal, no father that ever lived was happier than I, yet, I say the same thing now that I have said to you on many a previous occasion. The Emissions Guild should never have recommended that the Occult Bureau drop their investigation into what Manzini was doing at Industrial Plant No. 213. It is no coincidence that as soon as the matter was closed the Orphans of Doom appear out of nowhere, Xavier becomes chancellor, and we are at war in the Golden Triangle."

"And you believe these events are connected to one another, how?" said Princess Destiny.

"You know as well as I that Councilman Soros harbors a desire to annex the Golden Triangle as a province," said Governor Champagne. "He has discussed it with us on more than one occasion. His displeasure with my opposition to the idea was made abundantly clear. I am of the opinion that Councilman Soros used his power on the Supreme Council to ensure that a blind eye was turned to Xavier as he was allowed to use his fortune to rig our recent election in favor of himself so that once he was chancellor and had obtained his father's vacant seat, he could use his executive powers to lead us into the quagmire that the empire is now drowning ever so slowly in."

"Surely if it were true someone in the House of the Black Widow would have discovered this corruption and come forward," said Princess Destiny.

"He bought them all," said Governor Champagne. "Unlike Councilman Soros who has to go through me for every single dinar he desires, Xavier has his father's vast fortune and tryptamine investments at his disposal to do with as he pleases."

"These are serious allegations," said Princess Destiny.

"Did you ever stop to think," said Governor Champagne, "of how convenient it was that at the very moment the empire has an energy crisis and I refuse to back the annexation of the Golden Triangle, that suddenly, out of nowhere, the single biggest terrorist threat we have ever faced pops up in the middle of that coveted energy source?"

"I will admit I found it a rather odd coincidence," said Princess Destiny.

"You should have never supported the war," said Governor Champagne. "It sent the wrong message to every citizen of the empire."

"I have always looked upon war as a last resort," said Princess Destiny. "The tryptamine deposits in the Golden Triangle are greatly needed by our empire. I can not idly sit by and say nothing while a terrorist organization steals those resources right out from underneath us."

"Respectfully," said Governor Champagne, "I must disagree with your decision."

"I made my decision after many nights of prayer," said Princess Destiny. "It was only after meeting with Mystre that I made the choice that I did."

"Mystre," said Governor Champagne, "should never be trusted."

"He has been the spiritual adviser to my family since the day the Great Architect of the Universe cast Oblivion into the Void," said Princess Destiny. "Were it not for his wisdom and guidance who knows where we would be."

"It was Mystre who sent a servant girl to foolishly advise Oblivion to seek after the Jewel of Wisdom," said Governor Champagne. "I'm sure he wishes he would have done otherwise."

"Mystre studies the Codex Magicka day and night to find a way to restore our ancestors lost immortality to us," said Princess Destiny. "For that, I am eternally grateful."

"Who knows what he truly studies?" said Governor Champagne. "You can sit there and pretend all you want that you trust that evil creature, I, however, want nothing that he offers and have made peace with my mortality in the hopes that in the next life, if there be one, that therein I will be reunited one last time with Alexis' mother. Until that day, I will forever remind you that from the day I married her, to protect my family, I hide the truth from Mystre, under the constant threat of execution, that we are the followers of the Great Architect of the Universe and seek to cleanse the presence of the cults of the Priestess of Oblivion from what remains of the Gardens of Eternity."

"One cannot help but wonder why it was that the Great Architect of the Universe did not strip Mystre of his eternal life, nor punish him in any way?" said Princess Destiny.

"If your mind must wonder," said Governor Champagne, "let it seek out the answers to how we are to feed the hungry and heal the sick of our troubled empire."

"If your wife were here, she would have agreed with my decision," said Princess Destiny.

"I understand your desire to bring unity to our empire," said Governor Champagne. "I even admire your veiled attempt to use my family as a way to heal the troubles ailing it. I miss Alexis' mother. I won't lie about it. The longer she is gone, the deeper the pain of her loss becomes. You are right when you say that she would have agreed with your decision. The Golden Triangle was her home. Those are her people. A people, I'll remind you, that follow the Great Architect of the Universe, not Oblivion, or the cults of the evil bitch he calls a lover. But when it comes to Xavier, I cannot forgive him for what he did to Alexis. Nor would she. He is one of the largest shareholders in Controlled Substances Incorporated. Xavier bought his seat on their board of directors and single-handedly brought that company back from the brink of bankruptcy when he bailed it out with money from his own pocket. I know that for a fact because Giuseppe bragged about it to me before he died. Old Man Thorn went to his grave with a smile on his face knowing that his son had his hands around the throat of Manzini and his ailing operation. Chickenfeed was what he called what Xavier paid for it as though Manzini were a simple-minded beast whose loyalty was so easily earned it could be bought with what he tossed on the ground. There's no excuse for what happened. Xavier exposed Alexis to an untested and unreliable nekrobiotic that killed my only grandchild. I'll admit my corruption and the sorrow it has brought me. I didn't oppose their financial dealings when I thought it would benefit my daughter and her future family even though I knew that the holdings and investments of the Thorn family are in conflict with the office they hold, then, as they are now. Xavier like his father is chancellor of this empire. He owns the largest tryptamine mines in Zohar and profits from every stage of their harvesting, refinement, distribution, and sale. Thanks to his father being a founding member of the Imperial Central Bank and his inherited holdings he exerts an influence over that institution that is unequaled, and he is the largest shareholder in Controlled Substances Incorporated, second only to Manzini. The war in the Golden Triangle is nothing more than a war raged to enrich him and everyone around him."

Princess Destiny felt for Governor Champagne.

"As for your loss, I am truly sorry," she said in a dismayed voice. "But again, I must state the fact that you have no proof that it was Nekron that caused her to lose her unborn child nor that Xavier has ever used his families fortune for anything illegal. You took the same nekrobiotic, and yet here you sit, healthy."

"Surely you see the conflict of interest?" said Governor Champagne.

"I do," said Princess Destiny. "What I don't see is where he has broken any of the House of the Black Widow's, the Imperial Central Bank's, or the Supreme Council's rules on holding such investments. What his father did with his money and what Xavier is now doing, no matter how much we may disagree with it, at the end of the day, it is perfectly legal."

"My one eternal regret is that I should have never let Xavier near Alexis," said Governor Champagne. A great sadness rolled across his face. "Without his money, Manzini would have gone bankrupt long ago. His debts and addictions are secret to no one. It is my belief that Controlled Substances Incorporated created the Nekrobytes and that it was Xavier that gave them to the Orphans of Doom."

"What would you have me do?" said Princess Destiny.

"You have the power to override Councilman Soros on this issue," said Governor Champagne.

"The ruling of the Supreme Council is final," said Princess Destiny.

"Use your imperial veto," said Governor Champagne, "overturn their decision to seal my daughter's medical records and allow Professor Proxy to see what evidence may lay therein."

"You know that my position on the council is ceremonial," said Princess Destiny. "I am not an empress, nor do I wish to be."

"You inherited your father's imperial veto when he died," said Governor Champagne. "There would be no empire if it were not for him. Every member of the Supreme Council was placed there by his hand. One son or daughter from each of the Immortal Kingdoms to act as their emissary before the royal family of the Kingdom of Zohar, the land of the ziggurat and the ruins of the Temple of Oblivion."

"I miss him," said Princess Destiny.

"I miss King Roland, too," said Governor Champagne, "almost as much as I miss Alexis' mother. He was a good man and could have easily conquered the decaying Immortal Kingdoms and butchered everyone within their borders, yet he sought peace."

"The unification of all their kingdoms under one banner was his life's dream," said Princess Destiny. "My mother used to fight with him about it all the time. She hated the idea."

"Your father was lead astray by Mystre," said Governor Champagne, "and was fool enough to think it was a good idea to rebuild those accursed ruins for the Priestess of Oblivion with Giuseppe Thorn's money, where now, a handful of men and women oversee what remains of the ruination of this world as she hides in the shadows of the ziggurat. Everything they touch descends into chaos and yet here you sit, unworthy, to know the infernal secrets. Why is that?"

"My father would not speak of what he saw or learned in the presence of the Priestess of Oblivion," said Princess Destiny. "Why she now reveals herself only to Mystre, I do not know."

"Perhaps it is because she has something to hide?" said Governor Champagne.

Princess Destiny was silent for a moment. Her face became somber and then she said, "I'll be honest with you since we are far away from the ziggurat this evening. There is a part of me that is glad that I am not a part of her inner circle and the webs she weaves. Deep down inside I know the two of them are most likely up to no good. I dare not say this even in a whisper out of the fear that I may be heard by one of the Disciples of Oblivion and find myself murdered in some dark corner of the temple for letting it roll off my lips. Even now I fear that what I am saying is being listened to by one of the drones on duty this evening. The Throne of Oblivion is my prison. At times when I am in the presence of Mystre, I feel completely helpless. An intense fear rolls across my entire body as though he were trying to see my every thought, your families secret burdens my heart, but it is my father's memory that weighs heaviest on my mind. In my silence there are many times I wish he were still alive so that I could ask him what I should do or if he had to do it all over again would he do as you and instead of rebuilding the Lord of the Void his temple would he instead seek to wipe the cults of the Priestess of Oblivion from our land?"

"When your mother and father died of nekrosis," said Governor Champagne. "I wept for your loss, for I know how painful it was for me to lose my wife to that evil disease. Pain of that magnitude can cloud one's judgment almost as much as the prayers of Mystre. It is why the Occult Bureau's investigation into Industrial Plant No. 213 interested me as it did. I wanted an answer to why everyone around me was dying. In your father's absence you may have convinced yourself that your position is only ceremonial, perhaps it was Mystre or Councilman Soros that dared to plant that foolish notion in your head? Only you know its origin. I promised your father over many a fermented grape that I would tell you this. Never forget, it is you, Destiny Giavasis, that sits upon the Throne of Oblivion, no one else. You have one of two choices. You can either grow up and be the empress that your father raised you to be or you can die along with the empire that he founded. Your father kept his enemies close not so that they could rule the lands he unified but so that he could keep a bloodless watchful eye over every one of their corrupt ways as you should with Mystre and everything around him. Don't waste your time hoping the Supreme Council might one day come to their senses. I beg of you to use your imperial veto, no matter how ceremonial you think its authority may be. Send a signal to our people that you believe there is corruption taking place amongst the leadership of Controlled Substances Incorporated and that there will be a public investigation with full disclosure to every citizen as to what is going on at Industrial Plant No. 213. An investigation that should begin with the contents of my daughter's medical records."

The words of her father from the lips of Governor Champagne moved Princess Destiny.

"I had no idea that at the time of her health problems Alexis was pregnant," she said. "Why did you not tell me she was with child when she became ill? Why all the secrets?"

"That is something only Alexis can explain to you," said Governor Champagne. "It is not my place, but I will tell you this. After Alexis became ill, Professor Proxy ran a series of tests on her. In the blood samples of Alexis, he found Nekrobytes. During the analysis, the Nekrobytes in the blood samples of Alexis self-destructed and triggered some sort of reaction, not only amongst the Nekrobytes in her blood samples but in the ones that remained in her body as well. That is what almost killed her and landed her in the hospital. I know it to be true because I saw it with my own two eyes and it is the sole reason Councilman Soros wanted her medical records sealed and her blood samples seized. He did not want me to have any evidence that would back my claim. Nekron is poison. Trust me when I say this to you, Your Highness, the Supreme Council are a cabal so evil that the machinations of Councilman Soros are only exceeded by Oblivion when he conspired with the Divine Council to rebel against the Great Architect of the Universe."

"Did Professor Proxy test your blood as well?" said Princess Destiny.

"He did," said Governor Champagne.

"And what did he find?" said Princess Destiny.

"Nothing," said Governor Champagne. "It was his opinion that I could have received a placebo that was intended for Alexis and that it somehow was accidentally given to me instead."

Princess Destiny thought long and hard. Alexis was her best friend. The two of them had grown up together. They were sisters in all ways but blood. There was nothing that she would not do for her.

"I will grant your request," said Princess Destiny. "When next we meet with the Supreme Council, I will overturn their ruling and see to it that access to all of the medical records that pertain to Alexis are made available to you. Any other documents, or possible investigations, that have been sealed by the Occult Bureau, I will also inform the Supreme Council to make available to you as well. I want to know if there was a plot to take your life. If it is true, if there is some conspiracy lurking amongst our houses to harm you, or anyone around you, I want it uncovered and brought before me."

The words of Princess Destiny were a blessing to the ears of Governor Champagne.

"Thank you, Your Highness," he said. "I promise you that I would never do anything that would cause you to doubt my word or betray your trust."

"I know that my old friend," said Princess Destiny, "at times you have been like a father to me since my own passed away so many years ago. I know that if there is an honest and noble man left living amongst our people that I can trust and confide in, that it is you. But let me ask you one last final thing."

"What is it, Your Highness?" said Governor Champagne.

"What if Councilman Soros rejects my imperial veto of the Supreme Council's decision?" said Princess Destiny. "What will you do then?"

"I'll choke him to death with my bare hands if that's what it takes to find out the truth," said Governor Champagne.

Princess Destiny was shocked.

"They'll have you arrested for treason," she said.

"I don't care," said Governor Champagne.

5

ABRACADABRA'S ARCADE

Inside Abracadabra's Arcade, Alexis played her favorite video game, *Girls vs. Robots*. "Dead-gummit!" she said. Alexis kicked the coin-op. She'd died while trying to take out the final boss at the end of Level 8-4. Frustration continued to come in waves. Alexis held up her fingers in front of 808's visor like she was measuring something teeny-tiny. "I was this close to beating the game." With a look of disappointment on her face, she glanced back at the screen. *GAME OVER* was written across it. Alexis sighed, and said, "Oh, well. Let's get something to drink."

808 nodded in agreement.

The sounds of people laughing and enjoying themselves filled the arcade. They were playing the newest games in bajillions and bajillions of bits. 808 jumped up and looked over the shoulders of a few teenagers to see what games were new and popular amongst the youth of Zohar as he headed over to the concession stand with Alexis. When they got there, 808 ran over to a 1-up Energy Drink vending machine and looked at all the different flavors inside. 808 picked cherry, then swiped his black card engraved with the acronym S.C.R.I.L.L.A. on the front of it.

S.C.R.I.L.L.A. stood for Software, Computer, Real-Time, Interactive, Logistics, Language, Algorithm. It was the official digital currency of the Imperial Central Bank of the Black Sun Empire, known to the public as Scrilla.

Two, 1-up Energy Drinks, came out of the vending machine. 808 passed one to Alexis.

"Thank you," she said. They toasted. 808 took a sip of his energy drink. So did Alexis. She looked at her watch. "We need to get back to the Skybox. The fashion show is about to start."

808 guzzled his energy drink. After a final gulp, he threw it into a trash container next to a Microchips Potato Chips vending machine. They left the food court. Alexis and 808 were about to exit the arcade, when out of nowhere, Xavier blocked their path. His presence did not please Alexis, nor did it amuse 808.

"Get out of my way!" said Alexis.

Xavier wouldn't move.

"I want to talk to you," he said.

Alexis did her best to ignore him.

"I don't have anything to say to you," she said and tried to walk away.

808 looked up at Xavier like he was about to kill him.

Xavier reached out and grabbed Alexis by the arm.

"Stop!" he said.

Alexis pulled away from Xavier like she was about to have her purse snatched.

"Let me go!" she said.

Xavier lost his grip on her arm.

Alexis and 808 exited the arcade underneath a giant neon sign of the magician Abracadabra and his assistant Belladonna. Everyone in the Crystal Ball could hear the applause and cheers of the fashion show beginning as the models paraded up and down the catwalk in the latest bio-wearable clothing.

Alexis looked down at 808.

"We're going to miss it!" she said.

808 and Alexis ran as fast as they could toward the nearest elevator. A family was waiting in front of it. The sound of the elevator arriving rang out. The elevator door opened. Without warning, the Orphan of Doom inside triggered his suicide vest and detonated the explosives

strapped to his chest. The blast knocked Alexis and 808 flat on their backs.

Chaos engulfed everything around them.

Alexis shook 808. His ears were ringing. It took a few moments for 808's vision to come back into focus.

"Are you alright?" said Alexis. She had a cut on her forehead, and her hair was messed up

808 nodded his head that he was fine.

Tactical Drones swarmed into the Crystal Ball armed with Baphomet machine guns. Several canisters labeled *Nekrotek* hit the floor and infected everyone in the building unfortunate enough to come into contact with the nekrotik gas. Princess Destiny's honor guard placed a gas mask over her face and guided her out of the Skybox. The Orphans of Doom snaked their way through the ballroom and opened fire on the crowd. On their way to the Skybox, they killed all the board members on the board of directors of Controlled Substances Incorporated, the governors on the board of governors at the Imperial Central Bank, and the elected officials on the Emissions Guild. It was a bloodbath. The screams of dying people were all around Princess Destiny. She could not see Governor Champagne and feared that they might die at any moment.

Below them, on the mezzanine, Alexis and 808 ran up the stairwell to the floor her father was on. When they got there, they entered the Skybox only to find Governor Champagne kneeling execution style. Viirus was about to blow his head off.

"No!" screamed Alexis.

Viirus pulled the trigger on his handgun.

Blam!

Governor Champagne was dead. There was nothing Alexis could do. Viirus turned the gun on himself and committed suicide.

Blam!

The dead body of Viirus slumped to the floor next to Governor Champagne's. The Orphans of Doom, one by one, were killed by the swarming drones of the Occult Bureau until not a single one of them was alive. Alexis was about to run up to the body of her father when a Tactical Drone armed with a Circuit Breaker stun baton crept up behind her and hit her in the back of her head. Alexis was knocked out. Her limp body fell to the ground. Several Support Drones ran up to assist the Tactical Drone. One placed a gas mask over the face of Alexis. The Tactical Drone grabbed 808. 808 reached into his backpack. He pulled out a slingshot and fired a black galaxy marble right through the drone's visor. The Tactical Drone short-circuited and dropped 808. His whole body shook. 808 hit the floor. The Tactical Drone's head exploded. 808 looked around. The Support Drones were trying to kidnap Alexis. Two Medical Drones assisted them in moving her limp body out of the Skybox through an emergency exit. Without warning, an Enforcer Drone spotted 808 and the sizzling carcass of the Tactical Drone beside him. The Enforcer Drone fired a Trip Wire electronic net at 808. It missed him as 808 broke off into a full sprint and disappeared down the staircase of the Skybox and into a plume of smoke.

Outside of the Crystal Ball, the cameras of WXTZ Channel 13 were rolling. They were broadcasting the chaos and confusion LIVE to the citizens of the Black Sun Empire. Nekrotik gas and people were pouring out of the Crystal Ball. They trampled over one another as they choked to death and couldn't catch their breath. A fast-acting form of nekrosis was already beginning to set in. Some people were already bleeding out of their noses and mouths. The most pitiful ones in the crowd were already covered with sores and had gone blind. The few that had yet to show any signs or symptoms of contamination ran into the valet screaming and howling like wild animals, "Save us, please, save us! The Orphans of Doom have unleashed Nekrotek! Governor Champagne is dead!"

6

WXTZ CHANNEL 13

"WXTZ Channel 13 interrupts your regularly scheduled programming to bring you this special bulletin," said the voice of the announcer.

Johnny Lyes, the Black Sun Empire's most famous newsman, sat behind his desk while being powdered like a pampered slug. He was enjoying every minute of it. Johnny was an intellectual stump-monger of the lowest degree and highest magnitude, whose very presence anywhere he went, was enough to gag a maggotoid. A former bottom-feeding public access television broadcaster that preyed upon the ignorant, his rise to stardom had been both unexpected and sudden. Some said he'd sold his soul to Oblivion for his newfound fortune and fame. Others said he was working for the Occult Bureau. Regardless of what anyone may have said aloud, or thought to themselves, there was one thing that was for certain, his show, The Status Quo, dominated the news ratings amongst all the IPTV stations owned by the Black Nobility. The Status Quo's biggest sponsor was Controlled Substances Incorporated.

"We've just received word from the Crystal Ball that there has been an assassination attempt on the life of Governor Champagne," said Johnny Lyes. *"Lolita Sanchez is LIVE on the scene with more."*

Lolita Sanchez with her perked up boobs, and a heavy layer of clown make-up appeared on the television screens of the citizenry at home, at work, in the shops that lined Main Street, and that snaked their way through the Financial District.

"Johnny it has been confirmed that Governor Champagne is indeed dead after being brutally murdered by, Viirus, the leader of the terrorist organization, the Orphans of Doom," she said. *"General Grindcore has issued a statement that there is a citywide quarantine in effect and that the Orphans of Doom, did in fact, release Nekrotek during the attack. Every inhabitant of the city is to comply with a mandatory nekrobiotic inoculation."*

Meanwhile, in the ditch of the Super Highway, with his name slandered and clueless to what was going, Officer Whistle Britches found himself covered in soot and cryo-foam. Little did he know that Special Agent Scarzensky had already issued a press release stating that it was our tubby hero who'd allowed the Orphans of Doom to gain access to the Crystal Ball. Upon hearing those words broadcast to the four corners of what remained of the Gardens of Eternity, every citizen of the empire hated Officer Whistle Britches. He was a traitor, and they were glad to hear that he was dead. The smoke in the Podcaster smoldered to the point it was causing Officer Whistle Britches to choke every time he tried to take a breath. The Podcaster might have been goofy looking, but that didn't matter. Some of the strongest materials in the empire were used to craft that little car. It's why Officer Whistle Britches was still in one piece. He wiped the soot from his eyes and his vision came back into focus. Officer Whistle Britches was sore. His side hurt. He didn't have any cracked ribs. One of the Occult Bureau's Warlock patrol helicopters flew overhead. Officer Whistle Britches struggled to unfasten his seatbelt. When it came loose, he slumped out of his seat and crawled out of the wreckage of the Podcaster.

Floppy was almost lifeless.

"It's gonna be alright boy," said Officer Whistle Britches. "Just lay still."

Officer Whistle Britches dislodged his communicator from its docking station in the console of the Podcaster. He flipped it over. It was still on. Officer Whistle Britches scrolled across the shattered screen of the communicator to his recorded videos and hit the play icon on the video recorded that evening. What had just taken place in the loading dock of the Crystal Ball appeared on the screen of the communicator. The recording quality was perfect. There was nothing left to the imagination, nor did anything need to be interpreted. Officer Whistle Britches had caught Special Agent Scarzensky with a known terrorist moments before an attack on the Crystal Ball, and they'd tried to kill him for it. A look of determination appeared on his face. Officer Whistle Britches had to warn Alexis about what was about to happen. He opened his contacts app and scrolled down to Alexis' profile. The signal strength icon for Alexis showed, *Out of Service*. Officer Whistle Britches found that strange. He scrolled to 808's profile. 808 was still online. Officer Whistle Britches clicked 808's picture in an attempt to open up a communications link with him.

At the Crystal Ball, the alert message on 808's Grimoire went off. A picture of Officer Whistle Britches was on the screen. 808 hid behind a crate of nekrobiotics and pressed it.

"808, Special Agent Scarzensky and the Orphans of Doom, they're planning some kind of terrorist attack together!" shouted Officer Whistle Britches the moment he started streaming on the Grimoire's screen. *"You've got to warn Alexis and Governor Champagne!"*

808 motioned for him to be quiet and calm down. He typed out a text message that some drones kidnapped Alexis and that Governor Champagne was dead. Officer Whistle Britches was shocked. 808 typed that he was tracking Alexis and that he was on his way to get the Shadow Runner so that he could rescue her. He clicked the flip-camera button on his Grimoire. The camera on 808's Grimoire flipped and streamed a video of everything going on around him. General Grindcore's best mercenaries, Lieutenant Marcus Blood, Specialist Garcia Gutts, and Corporal Ricardo Gore were overseeing the mandatory inoculations. They'd just finished loading the body of Viirus into the back of an Imperial Transport marked for disposal. Medical Drones stacked crates of Nekron next to a triage center. There was more than enough of the nekrobiotic to go around. If you didn't want to get probed, poked, pinched, tackled, searched, stripped, manhandled, arrested, shot, or killed, you didn't say, do, suggest, or even hint that you might be thinking of noncompliance. Most of the citizens that had been inside during the attack were doing what they were told to do. There were a few hold-outs though that knew something wasn't right. Two and two weren't making four, and they

wanted some answers. One hold-out refused to co-operate with the mandatory inoculation. That was the wrong thing to do.

"I've got rights! I ain't taking that nekrobiotic!" shouted the citizen refusing to be stuck with a needle. Several Enforcer Drones proceeded to beat him down with Circuit Breakers for not complying with a direct order. A riot broke out around them.

"I'm sending you my location," said Officer Whistle Britches in a state of utter disbelief. A map appeared in the upper right-hand corner of the screen of 808's Grimoire. *"I need you to come and pick me up."*

808 ended the transmission. He took a vial of Nekron out of the crate he was hiding behind and put it in his backpack. 808 peeped around the corner of the crate. The coast was clear. He ran across the street as fast as he could toward the parking garage of the Crystal Ball. Once there, he ran inside and up to the second level where the Shadow Runner's tracking device signaled to him its current location. 808 peaked around the corner to make sure that the coast was clear. It wasn't. A robotic bomb-sniffing dog patrolled the level. The collar around its neck read, *Killer*. A Security Drone led him passed several parked cars and was about to lead him up to the next level. 808 crept toward the Shadow Runner. Beside him, a rat scurried along the top of one of the cement walls. It nicked an empty 1-up Energy Drink can that fell to the ground next to 808.

"Rrrrrrr!" growled Killer. He turned and spotted 808.

808 bolted for the Shadow Runner. The Security Drone unleashed Killer. In a blind panic, 808 kept slipping and falling like he was running through a nightmare. Killer was almost on him when he got to the Shadow Runner. 808 put his hand on the window. The window of the Shadow Runner scanned his hand. It recognized his fingerprints just in time to unlock. 808 jumped inside. When he shut the door, Killer pounced and hit the closed door at full speed. Killer couldn't get inside. He proceeded to claw the paint off of the exterior of the vehicle. 808 threw the Shadow Runner into drive. He slammed the power pedal to the floor. The Shadow Runner raced off of the level it was parked on and out of the parking garage. A tracking device in the necklace of Alexis alerted 808 to the direction she was traveling in. 808 merged onto the loop that encircled the Crystal Ball and circled around to the back of the Crystal Ball's property. In a few moments, he was

running parallel with the drainage ditch Officer Whistle Britches was climbing out of.

Professor Proxy appeared on a monitor built into the dashboard of the Shadow Runner.

"808 are you alright?" he said. *"I've been trying to contact you. Where's Alexis? There are reports all over the IPTV networks that she murdered her father."*

808 didn't say anything. His thoughts dictated themselves out one character at a time across the screen in Professor Proxy's lab along with all of the video he'd recorded with his visor while inside of the Crystal Ball. A particular piece of video containing Viirus caught Professor Proxy's eye. He zoomed in on the video. The enhanced footage came into focus. Professor Proxy couldn't help but notice that a full-grown Nekrobyte ran out of the bullet hole in Viirus' skull. Both 808 and Professor Proxy found it strange that a Nekrobyte that size would have been inside Viirus while he was still healthy and alive.

It wasn't long until 808 spotted Officer Whistle Britches. 808 rolled down the front passenger side window. Officer Whistle Britches saw the Shadow Runner. He waved at it. The internal heads-up display on 808's visor indicated that Floppy was still in the ditch. His power levels were low. 808 slowed down the Shadow Runner. Officer Whistle Britches ran up to the front passenger side window.

"I saw it all, 808!" he said. Officer Whistle Britches was so excited that he didn't realize he was yelling. Officer Whistle Britches opened the front passenger side door of the Shadow Runner and plopped inside.

808 clicked a button labeled *R.O.V.E.R.* on the center console of the Shadow Runner. R.O.V.E.R. stood for Remote, Online, Vehicle, Evacuation, Robot. A small-wheeled medical robot dropped from the bottom of the car and rolled down into the ditch next to the Super Highway. Back in the Shadow Runner, 808's optics focused on the video in front of him. Sho'nuff, Officer Whistle Britches recorded everything. 808 enhanced his view, then pulled out a stylus that looked like a black crayon. On his Grimoire, he wrote something down. 808 handed the Grimoire to Officer Whistle Britches.

"Put your seatbelt on," said Officer Whistle Britches as he read aloud what 808 had written on his Grimoire. 808 mashed the power pedal of the Shadow Runner to the floor. Officer Whistle Britches was sucked deep into his seat. He scrambled for his seat belt as they raced off down the Super Highway and he shouted, "Hey! Don't forget about Floppy!" 808 hadn't forgotten about him. While he was scribbling down his message to Officer Whistle Britches on his Grimoire, the Rover loaded Floppy into the trunk of the Shadow Runner. The computer system in the Shadow Runner uploaded a damage report to the servers monitored by Professor Proxy at Zohar University along with a copy of the video Officer Whistle Britches had just shown 808. Professor Proxy appeared on the internal heads-up display on 808's visor. He couldn't believe what just streamed before his eyes. The footage of Viirus was enough to boggle the mind, but the fact that Special Agent Scarzensky was with him just moments before the attack, well, that was insane.

Down the road, inside the Imperial Prisoner Transportation Unit carrying Alexis, she sat alone fighting off the waves of depression and constant thoughts of hopelessness that filled her mind. Scarzensky's Roach ran along the ceiling undetected. Alexis sat handcuffed in Charm Bracelets. Her necklace hung down between her legs. She was slumped over with her elbows resting on her knees. Her heart-shaped locket opened to reveal a picture of her with Xavier. She still loved him. She'd always love him.

Outside, with 808 still behind the wheel, the Shadow Runner raced up beside the Imperial Prisoner Transportation Unit. Alexis' contact lenses synced with the heads-up display in the Shadow Runner. 808 could see everything going on inside the Imperial Prisoner Transportation Unit. Everything she saw, he saw. A sign signaling that Exit-610 onto the Super Highway was fast approaching. 808 mashed the power pedal to the floor and raced out in front of the Imperial Prisoner Transportation Unit. The Shadow Runner dropped a Minion EMP landmine down into the road. It exploded. The Imperial Prisoner Transportation Unit wobbled and kept rolling. It was obvious that the transportation unit had an extra set of EMP proof armor that shielded it from small arms EMP attacks.

808 motioned for Officer Whistle Britches to take the wheel. The steering wheel slid across the dashboard and came to rest in front of Officer Whistle Britches lap. Officer Whistle Britches took control of the

Shadow Runner. 808 reached underneath his seat and pulled out two Uzi's, the MK Ultra Mark I and the MK Ultra Mark II. 808 rolled down his window and from over the top of the Shadow Runner, he opened fire on the driver side window of the Imperial Prisoner Transportation Unit. The windows of the transportation unit shattered. The Logistics Drone behind the wheel burst into flames. The Imperial Prisoner Transportation Unit swerved and tipped over on its side. It slid across the road. Sparks flew everywhere. The Imperial Prisoner Transportation Unit hit a guardrail. Once it was no longer moving, Alexis crawled out of the back of the Imperial Prisoner Transportation Unit. Officer Whistle Britches pulled up beside it. 808 jumped out of the Shadow Runner and ran over to Alexis to see if she was injured.

"You alright?" said Officer Whistle Britches.

Alexis bent over to catch her breath.

"Yeah, I'm fine," she said. Scarzensky's Roach crawled up one of the Shadow Runner's tires and underneath a seat in the car. "I just got the wind knocked out of me."

In the distance, a swarm of Enforcer Drones driving Stalkers raced toward the wrecked Imperial Prisoner Transportation Unit.

"Looks like we've got company," said Officer Whistle Britches.

"Come on," said Alexis to 808. "Let's get out here."

7

HOUSE OF THE BLACK WIDOW

Outside of the House of the Black Widow, an angry mob was beginning to form at the front steps where Supreme Council Resolution 33 would soon be passed into law. A brick thrown by an agitator with hands covered in nekrotik chancres bounced off the riot shield of a Security Drone. It didn't leave a scratch. A mercenary in the Imperial Armada opened fire with a Suffocator riot control weapon. Canisters rained down on the crowd. Some feared that there might be Nekrotek inside the canisters and not tear gas. The mob gasped for their breath. Security Drones moved in with their Circuit Breakers. One by one they beat everyone in their path senseless. General Grindcore and the Think Tanks of the Imperial Armada locked down the area. Pitch Shifters emerged from the sides of the Imperial Think Tanks and began playing a warning message.

"*Attention, attention, attention. The Imperial Armada is here to help. Remain calm. By executive order, Chancellor Thorn declares this to be an unlawful assembly. Civil disobedience will not be tolerated. All those assembled are ordered to disperse immediately. If you remain, you will be subject to arrest.*"

Inside the House of the Black Widow, the Marquis Van Gogh, the minority leader of the Checkmate Club, banged a gavel and did his best to quiet the members of both parties in attendance.

"Order! Order!" he shouted. It was useless. No one would listen to him. It was Xavier they feared. The members of the Checkmate Club and the Brimstone Society continued arguing amongst one another. It was a madhouse. They were scared. The mob outside would not disperse. A full blown riot had erupted and was being broadcast for the whole crumbling empire to see. Nekrosis spread amongst everyone with whom they coughed or touched. Rumors of overrun mercenaries on duty at the refugee camps scattered throughout the city began to surface. During a report that Alexis aided Officer Whistle Britches and the Orphans of Doom in the assassination attempt on her father, WXTZ Channel 13 announced that Chancellor Thorn had given the command to General Grindcore to use lethal force against the crowd rioting outside of the House of the Black Widow. The carnage streamed into the home and workplace of every citizen. It was beyond description.

In the foyer, Princess Destiny was waiting with her honor guard for Xavier to arrive. She paced in front of the doors that led into the House of the Black Widow's innermost chamber. Like all of her subjects, she'd seen the report about Alexis and Officer Whistle Britches aiding the Orphans of Doom in their assassination attempt on Governor Champagne. She couldn't believe it. Governor Champagne's warning earlier in the evening haunted her mind.

Xavier appeared guarded by a dozen centurions in the Order of the Trapezoid and a small swarm of Security Drones.

Princess Destiny approached him.

"Chancellor Thorn, if I might have a word?" she said.

The centurions stood ready to attack Princess Destiny's honor guard if they made any sudden moves. Xavier waved them off. She was no threat to him.

"Yes, Your Highness," said Xavier.

"I would like to speak with you about what I just heard concerning Alexis," said Princess Destiny.

Alexis was the last thing Xavier wanted to discuss. He'd just finished speaking with Special Agent Scarzensky about her. Xavier wanted her safe and away from all the carnage at the Crystal Ball. Instead, Special Agent Scarzensky informed him that not only had she escaped the Occult Bureau's custody, but that his battle androids had botched the murder of Officer Whistle Britches as well, and that he'd had a hand in freeing her.

"What of her?" said Xavier.

"I have yet to be briefed by either yourself or the Supreme Council on the particulars concerning the assassination of Governor Champagne," said Princess Destiny. "I have a hard time believing Alexis was involved in her father's death."

Xavier looked at Princess Destiny like an inquisitive child.

"It was Alexis," he said, "that instructed Officer Whistle Britches to allow the Orphans of Doom to gain access to the Crystal Ball and who let Viirus into the Skybox in which her father sat. You saw her excuse herself earlier in the evening. She was angry with Governor Champagne and—"

"That is not what I saw at all!" said Princess Destiny.

"We have surveillance footage provided by the Occult Bureau that shows Alexis and Officer Whistle Britches not only allowing the Orphans of Doom access to the facility but providing them with the weaponry with which they launched their attack," said Xavier.

"Chancellor Thorn," said Princess Destiny in an annoyed tone. She knew she was being lied to and did not appreciate being treating like a simpleton. "I demand you show me this footage at once."

"The Supreme Council has sealed the footage in the interest of imperial security," said Xavier.

"I will not stand for this!" said Princess Destiny.

Xavier had grown tired of Princess Destiny's belly-aching.

"Unless you want to find yourself on a psychiatric hold at the request of the Supreme Council," he said. "I would be careful with whom you mention this conversation. For if you are foolish enough to decide to do so, I can assure you that there is nothing I will be able to do to save you from the wrath of Councilman Soros. Do we understand each other?"

Princess Destiny's blood began to boil.

"Indeed, we do," she said.

8

SUPREME COUNCIL RESOLUTION 33

Two centurions in the Order of the Trapezoid opened the doors to the chamber where the members of the House of the Black Widow now sat in obeisance.

"Members of the House of the Black Widow," said the Marquis Van Gogh, "I have the high privilege and distinct honor of presenting to you Xavier Thorn, Chancellor of the Black Sun Empire."

Xavier entered the chamber.

The members of the House of the Black Widow rose from their seats. Everyone in attendance applauded Xavier. The cameras of the IPTV networks and WXTZ Channel 13 were fixed upon him so that all throughout the Black Sun Empire could hear his words. Xavier approached the podium.

"Citizens of the Black Sun Empire and distinguished members of the House of the Black Widow," he said. "It is with a saddened and heavy heart, amidst an ever-worsening refugee crisis, that I come before you. As you all well know, earlier this evening, a former member of this great body was murdered in cold blood. Murdered by a terrorist organization that he thought to be an insignificant and minor threat, not only to himself but to our collective empire. A threat that corrupted his own daughter into aiding his murderers in his assassination and that caused one of our law enforcement officials to betray the trust of the very citizens he swore to protect.

"For far too long we have allowed the Orphans of Doom, and those like them, to infect the body politic of not only this empire but our families as well. All because of the inability of only one amongst us who would not do what needed to be done, and now, because of that error in judgment, not only has he paid the ultimate price, but many innocent people now lay dead by his side as well. Who will be next? Who will be the next one that falters when looking out for the best interest of our people so that they can be murdered before our very eyes because we did not have the political will to see the Orphans of Doom for what they are and be willing to stand united together against them?

"Make no mistake about it. The Orphans of Doom are the biggest threat to this empire and its safety and security that we as a people have ever seen. In a message found streaming online after the attack, in one of the far corners of the dark web obtained by the Occult Bureau, Viirus, the leader of the Orphans of Doom, took credit for the attack. He bragged that the chemical weapon, known as Nekrotek, was detonated, releasing the contagion that causes the disease known as nekrosis, throughout the Crystal Ball, and thereby infecting almost everyone therein. Was it not for Controlled Substances Incorporated making its new nekrobiotic, Nekron, freely available, neither I nor anyone else in attendance would be alive and standing here this evening.

"The Nekrotek induced disease, nekrosis, as I speak to you now, is spreading throughout the city of Zohar by those that have already refused to comply with the mandatory nekrobiotic inoculation program. Because of this threat, I have taken emergency executive authority and ordered General Grindcore to institute a city-wide quarantine. No one is to attempt to leave, nor enter the capital.

"It is at this time that I would like to address those that have begun to riot in our streets and who have chosen to refuse to comply with my executive order to restore peace to this city. Let there be no doubt that the Orphans of Doom were responsible and admit to the murder of one of the greatest leaders that the Black Sun Empire has ever known. Who knows how many of them remain hidden amongst us? Even now as I speak to you, the Orphans of Doom lay in wait, disguised as refugees, and are ready to strike again. Viirus is still out there with them, plotting the death of not only the empire but our way of life."

Xavier no more had the word, *life*, out of his mouth when a small group of young men and women shouted, "Death to the House of the Black Widow! Death to Occult Bureau! Death to the Imperial Armada!" The cameras of the IPTV networks and WXTZ Channel 13 zoomed-in on the group of young men and women the moment their disturbance echoed throughout the chamber. The members of the House of the Black Widow rustled in their seats and chattered amongst themselves. No one knew how the group of young men and women had gained access to the chamber. Even worse, they thought to themselves as they were arrested and hauled off by several centurions, what if they'd detonated a dirty bomb laced with Nekrotek? Little did they know that it was all a show for the cameras. The group of young men and women in question were undercover agents in the employ of the Occult Bureau disguised as civilian protesters. Xavier had arranged the whole charade in advance with Special Agent Scarzensky. It worked. The members of the House of the Black Widow now feared for their safety and their lives. Not a single soul amongst them wanted to end up like Governor Champagne, a corpse.

"My fellow legislators, this is the kind of madness of which I speak!" said Xavier. "Are we safe and secure within our halls of government or are we not? We cannot continue to tolerate non-violent extremists that include conspiracy theorists and those that would deny that the Orphans of Doom were behind the terrorist attack at the Crystal Ball this evening. They are just as dangerous to this empire and its people as the Orphans of Doom. I beg of you and plead upon the Throne of Oblivion that you allow yourselves to come to the sickening realization, that something, anything, must be done about the lawlessness of this empire. You must realize before it is too late, that a criminal element amongst us, has become so brazen, that they would openly plot and brag about the premeditated murder of one of our very own. They would do this while unleashing a plague upon all of our houses. A plague that would see our empire rot from within like the corpse of a dead animal left to putrefy on the side of the road! Now I ask you, who among you can condone such an act of violence?

"Supreme Council Resolution 33, can and will enable, not only the Occult Bureau but the entire military might of the Imperial Armada to do one thing and one thing only, clean up our streets and make them safe again, not only for our children but for every decent family and hardworking citizen in the whole of the Black Sun Empire. Their presence must be made permanent so that we can see to it that every single inhabitant of the city of Zohar, bar none, receives a nekrobiotic inoculation to eradicate the threat of nekrosis from spreading amongst us. We need them now, more than ever. Will you join me?"

The members of the House of the Black Widow, both the Brimstone Society and the Checkmate Club, rose to their feet in a bipartisan show of unity and clapped their hands as hard as they could. It was a roaring, standing ovation of approval, almost deafening. Not a single one of them would vote nay in objection to Supreme Council Resolution 33. Without the opposition of Governor Champagne there to stop them, Xavier and Councilman Soros got what they wanted. Supreme Council Resolution 33, was now the law of the land.

9

ZOHAR UNIVERSITY

Inside Zohar University, Professor Proxy was seated at a workstation in his lab when Alexis, 808, Officer Whistle Britches, and a damaged Floppy arrived. The Rover from the Shadow Runner placed Floppy on an examination table.

"He's hurt pretty bad," said Officer Whistle Britches. He was well acquainted with Professor Proxy having worked as a security guard at the university before being accepted into the ranks of the Occult Bureau.

"I've read the damage report," said Professor Proxy as he got up from his seat at the workstation he was at and approached the examination table.

"We're lucky to be alive," said Officer Whistle Britches.

Professor Proxy looked over Floppy.

"And, how are you doing?" said Professor Proxy as he glanced up at Alexis with a look of concern on his face.

"I'm fine," said Alexis.

"You sure?" said Professor Proxy.

"I said, I'm fine," said Alexis.

"Alright, I believe you," said Professor Proxy. He left Floppy's side at the examination table and walked over to his desk. Professor Proxy unlocked the top drawer and pulled out an envelope.

"However, I've got something here for you that I'm sure you'll want to see."

"What is it?" said Alexis.

"A letter from your father," said Professor Proxy. "He instructed me to give it to you if anything were to ever happen to him."

Alexis took the envelope from Professor Proxy and opened it. Professor Proxy pulled up a stool and sat down beside the examination table. He initialized a diagnostic test to make sure that there was no permanent damage done to Floppy.

"Can you fix him?" said Officer Whistle Britches, still worried more about Floppy than himself.

"Sure, it'll take a little time," said Professor Proxy, "but when I'm done with him, he'll be as good as new."

808 pulled out the vial of Nekron from his backpack and placed it on the examination table next to the hand of Professor Proxy.

"And, this is?" he said.

"That is a vial of Nekron manufactured by Controlled Substances Incorporated," said Alexis.

Scarzensky's Roach ran up the wall behind Professor Proxy. He lifted up his glasses and examined the vial. The computer equipment in the lab scrambled the roach's signal.

"Where did you get this?" said Professor Proxy.

"The Crystal Ball," said Alexis.

Professor Proxy booted up his sequencing software and extracted the contents of the vial into a syringe. Professor Proxy injected the Nekron into a lab rat. A vast array of hi-tech lab equipment analyzed its vital signs, Professor Proxy's monitor filled with information. Alexis could tell by the expression on his face he'd found something.

"What is it?" she said.

Analysis: Synthetic Lifeform...

Tag Identification Complete...

Sequence Number: 00593

Origin: Industrial Plant No. 213

"Nanobots," said Professor Proxy, "but none like I've ever seen before."

"What are nanobots doing in a nekrobiotic?" said Officer Whistle Britches.

"I don't know," said Professor Proxy. "I was expecting to find Nekrobytes. But I do know this. The nanobots are grafting something to the rat's DNA. Here, take a look."

Professor Proxy streamed what he saw onto the screen of a large monitor in front of Alexis, 808, and Officer Whistle Britches. He zoomed in on the nanobots so that they could get a better look.

"The origin stamp on this batch of nanobots is Industrial Plant No. 213," said Alexis. "That's the Death Factory."

"Indeed, it is," said Professor Proxy.

"There aren't any Nekrobytes present at all?" said Alexis.

"None," said Professor Proxy.

"What are they working on?" said Alexis.

"It looks like a neurotransmitter to me," said Professor Proxy. "But at this stage in its creation, it's too early to tell what it is."

"How long do you think it'll take before you know for sure?" said Alexis.

"A couple of hours," said Professor Proxy.

Alexis thought for a moment and looked down at 808.

"We need to get inside the Death Factory and see why Manzini's putting nanobots in his nekrobiotics," she said. "If we can gain access to Controlled Substances Incorporated's mainframe, there's no telling what we'll learn about Nekron."

Officer Whistle Britches knew she was right.

"The only way to get in there undetected is through the entrance to the sewer system on the western side of Bayou Beignet," he said. "Turtlehead Creek opens up right at the lagoon where Manzini dumps most of the factories toxic waste."

"Are you sure of this?" said Alexis.

"Sure, I'm sure," said Officer Whistle Britches. "I used to be a security guard there. One of the largest sewer pipes they've got is wide-open and unguarded so that they can dump massive amounts of chemicals from inside the factory anytime they want. It's easy to get inside that way if you're willing to risk your health. You could drive a boat right through it, but the real question is where are you going to get one?"

"I might know of a pirate or two that can lend a hand when it comes to a boat," said Alexis.

"I take it you're referring to Junebug and Minx?" said Professor Proxy.

"I am," said Alexis.

"They'd be perfect for the job," said Professor Proxy.

"Last I heard, Junebug was spending most of his time with Minx down at the Fleur De Lis," said Alexis. "It's been a while since I've seen or spoken to either of them."

808 walked across the lab toward a Synaptic Terminal. When he arrived at the terminal, he climbed inside to recharge his power cells.

"Looks like 808 needs a tune-up," joked Officer Whistle Britches.

Professor Proxy walked over to the Synaptic Terminal. He initiated a diagnostic systems test.

"Have you been taking your nootropics?" said Professor Proxy. 808 nodded his head yes. Professor Proxy looked over 808's nutrient and vitamin levels. "Your iodine levels look a little low."

"What's he take iodine for, I thought he was a robot?" said Officer Whistle Britches.

"He is, but he's also part human," said Professor Proxy.

Officer Whistle Britches couldn't believe it.

"Get out of here," he said.

Professor Proxy walked over to his medicine cabinet and took out a bottle of iodine.

"No, there's a little boy in there," he replied.

Professor Proxy gave the bottle of iodine to 808.

"Who's his mother?" said Officer Whistle Britches.

Professor Proxy was hesitant to say anything. Alexis looked at the two of them in a coy silence. Officer Whistle Britches could tell that the two of them had a secret between them.

"It's okay," said Alexis. "You can tell him."

"Tell me what?" said Officer Whistle Britches.

"Alexis is his mother," said Professor Proxy.

Officer Whistle Britches was dumbfounded.

"You're his mother?" he said.

Alexis looked over at 808 with a smile on her face that only a mother can have.

"Yep, that's my baby boy inside there," she said. "He's my pride and joy."

"He's a miracle of science," said Professor Proxy.

"So," said Officer Whistle Britches with a confused look on his face, "how'd he end up a robot?"

"I took some Nekron in a refugee camp I was visiting," said Alexis. "It caused me to have a miscarriage."

"Why did you do that?" said Officer Whistle Britches.

"Everyone in the Golden Triangle knows my mother died of nekrosis," said Alexis, "so when I heard that Controlled Substances Incorporated had a potential cure I told Xavier that I'd help to demonstrate to the people living in the refugee camps that it was safe. They thought it would kill them, so to prove that it wouldn't, I allowed myself to receive an inoculation just like they would. My father went with me because he'd lived with my mother in the Golden Triangle when they first married. He knew the territory and the people very well. They trusted him."

"What was in the Nekron that caused you to have a miscarriage?" said Officer Whistle Britches.

"Nekrobytes," said Alexis.

"There were Nekrobytes in the Nekron distributed in the Golden Triangle?" said Officer Whistle Britches. "Who put them in there the Orphans of Doom?"

"No," said Alexis. "My father believed that someone at Controlled Substances Incorporated put them in the nekrobiotic and that the lethal dose I was given was intended for him."

"Your father believed someone at Controlled Substances Incorporated was trying to kill him?" said Officer Whistle Britches.

"It looks that way," said Professor Proxy.

"Who'd he think did it?" said Officer Whistle Britches.

"He believed Xavier was responsible for it," said Alexis.

"Chancellor Thorn?" said Officer Whistle Britches.

"He's one of the largest investors in the company," said Professor Proxy. "It would have been impossible for him not to know what was going on."

"That's bonkers," said Officer Whistle Britches. "It could have been Carlyle Manzini, Dr. Necropolis, or even an Orphan of Doom that managed to infiltrate the company. Why would Chancellor Thorn do something so stupid? He would have ruined himself, bankrupted the company, possibly lost a fortune in the process. Not to mention he'd be executed or thrown into a containment cube for the rest of his life if he was caught. Publicly killing your father with a tainted nekrobiotic that could be traced back to him, it doesn't make any sense. I mean come on, the two of you were engaged to be married. What did he possibly have to gain from such an idiotic decision?"

"That's what we've been trying to figure out," said Professor Proxy.

"Do you have any of the Nekrobytes as evidence?" said Officer Whistle Britches.

"They self-destructed when Professor Proxy tried to remove them from one of my blood samples," said Alexis.

"Geez, Louise," said Officer Whistle Britches. "I believe you when you say there were Nekrobytes. It's just that it's a story so far-fetched I don't know how anybody else would believe you without any evidence."

"The Supreme Council decreed that all of her medical records and blood samples were to be seized in the interest of imperial security," said Professor Proxy. "Neither myself nor Governor Champagne, not even Alexis, was allowed to examine them."

"You weren't allowed to view your medical records?" said Officer Whistle Britches.

"Nope," said Alexis. "They claimed whatever was in my body, if anything was in my body, was the property of Controlled Substances Incorporated."

"That would have included 808," said Professor Proxy. "When the Nekrobytes self-destructed, Alexis went into labor. Governor Champagne had me hide him out of the fear that if the Supreme Council learned that he'd lived and got their hands on him, they'd have him destroyed. The boy was very sick during the transition into his new body. Xavier knew all of this and still refused to help."

"So Chancellor Thorn knows his son's alive?" said Officer Whistle Britches.

"Yes," said Alexis. "But he refuses to acknowledge his existence. In Xavier's mind, our son died the moment I miscarried. He refuses to accept that the Nekrobytes completely altered 808's physiology, and yet somehow he lived. It's a difficult thing to live with as a parent, but the fact of the matter is that Professor Proxy used an experimental drone technology to house our son's body before it wasted away. Once 808 was inside, his nekrobiotic biology fused with his new cybernetic body and he became what I can only describe a new nekrogenetic species. A hybrid lifeform made out of man, machine, and Nekrobyte."

"Why'd ya'll name him 808?" said Officer Whistle Britches.

"I made his body from a mold of Drone Project 808," said Professor Proxy.

"How far along were you when you had him?" said Officer Whistle Britches.

"Six months," said Alexis. "It's been almost a year since I took the Nekron."

"808's eighteen months old?" said Officer Whistle Britches.

"Give or take a week or two," said Alexis.

"Wait a second," said Officer Whistle Britches, "you gave an eighteen-month-old an Uzi?"

"With the aid of the cybernetic drone software in his armor he learns at an accelerated rate that boggles the mind," said Professor Proxy.

"You don't give an eighteen-month-old an Uzi!" said Officer Whistle Britches. "I don't care what kind of software he's running!"

"You need to calm down," said Alexis.

"You should have told me what was going on," said Officer Whistle Britches. "If the Supreme Council didn't have them destroyed I could have used the Occult Bureau's workstations to locate your medical records."

"I was scared something might happen to 808 if I told too many people," said Alexis. "As a mother, I felt that my family was safer if everyone thought I'd lost him. I'm sorry for all the secrecy, but it's something I had to do."

Officer Whistle Britches felt that it might be rude to inquire any further into the personal life of his friend. The awkward silence soon found itself broken when 808 exited the Synaptic Terminal.

Diagnostic Systems Test Complete...

All Systems Are Fully Functional...

System Power At 100%...

808 walked to the other side of the lab and on a large monitor the size of a chalkboard he drew the Golden Ratio. When the drawing was

complete, it disappeared, and a command prompt appeared. It requested the pin number of the monitor. 808 typed in 1618. The monitor flipped open and revealed a hidden room. 808 walked inside. It was a small armory. 808 removed the MK Ultra Mark I & II from his backpack and began to service his weapons.

Atop an R&D Station used for crafting new experimental weapons and the mods attached to them, a calculator watch caught the eye of Officer Whistle Britches. It was glowing in an isolation chamber.

"What kind of watch is that?" said Officer Whistle Britches.

"That's a DDT," said Professor Proxy.

Officer Whistle Britches looked puzzled.

"Kinda looks like a calculator watch to me," he said. "Why do you call it a DDT? That the brand name or something?"

"Because if you get hit with it, and survive, you're going to feel like you just got DDT'd," said Professor Proxy.

"You've got brain damage," said Officer Whistle Britches. "You know that right?"

"Check it out," said Professor Proxy with a grin. He unlocked the isolation chamber and handed the DDT to Officer Whistle Britches. "All you have to do is type in 3141 to unlock it."

Officer Whistle Britches strapped the DDT around his wrist and typed 3141 on its screen. The DDT unlocked and transformed the calculator watch into a giant hand cannon.

"What the heck?" Officer Whistle Britches muttered under his breath.

"The DDT gathers the energy around you to create a torsion field," said Professor Proxy. "It uses the torsion field not only to attack your enemies but slow down time as well."

Officer Whistle Britches didn't believe him.

"I'm calling bullshit," he said.

"For real. But it's only for a tiny fraction of a second. You can take some target practice over here," said Professor Proxy. He motioned to what looked like a big black diamond floating in the air. "Fire into the monolith. It will absorb the DDT's energy without anyone getting hurt."

Officer Whistle Britches pulled the trigger of the DDT.

Bah-dooooooommmm!

The blast lifted Officer Whistle Britches off the ground and blew him clear across the room.

Professor Proxy snapped his fingers.

"I knew I forgot something," he said. Professor Proxy ran to a shelf on the opposite side of the room. There he grabbed a pair of boots, then ran back across the room, and presented them to Officer Whistle Britches. He was almost unconscious with tweety-birds flying around his head. "Make sure you have on these."

Officer Whistle Britches shook his head.

"Boots?" he said, once he came to his senses.

"They're Gravity Boots," said Professor Proxy. "They'll give you a center of gravity when you fire the DDT."

"Why didn't you tell me that before?" said Officer Whistle Britches.

"I forgot," said Professor Proxy.

"I could have broken my neck!" said Officer Whistle Britches.

"Just be sure to have on the Gravity Boots the next time you pull the trigger," said Professor Proxy. "Also, give the DDT a few seconds to cool down and recharge after every blast. Otherwise, nothing will come out."

Officer Whistle Britches was so mad that he tried to shoot Professor Proxy with the DDT. He clicked the trigger over and over again, but it wouldn't fire. Professor Proxy smiled while Alexis fastened an Enigma handgun to each thigh, stuck a pair of Ionic Daggers in her boots for safekeeping, and looked at the two of them like they were crazy.

10

IPTV

All over the Black Sun Empire, the descendants of the Flower Children were watching a prerecorded confession of Viirus taking responsibility for the night's terrorist attack at the Crystal Ball when the broadcast was interrupted by Lolita Sanchez and the cameras of WXTZ Channel 13 as they streamed LIVE from behind a fenced security barrier. Princess Destiny and Xavier had arrived at the ziggurat via Warlock helicopters with the inner circle of the Black Nobility whose fortunes and bloodlines were a who's-who of the elite members of both parties of the House of the Black Widow initiated into the higher degrees of the cults of the Priestess of Oblivion. General Grindcore and his staff escorted the inner circle of the Black Nobility, Princess Destiny, and her honor guard into the ziggurat. She wanted to speak to the reporters but was not permitted. Across the city, only a few miles from where they were now, the rest of the members of the Checkmate Club and the Brimstone Society of lesser degrees had been left to die. Rioters overran the barricades of the Imperial Armada after the completion of the vote to approve Supreme Council Resolution 33. They set fire to the House of the Black Widow. The news sent shockwaves throughout the empire.

Councilman Soros was pleased with how the chaos of the evening was beginning to unfold. The Imperial Armada accompanied by the

Occult Bureau's drones were going door to door to ensure that every inhabitant of the city of Zohar was inoculated with Nekron. Millions refused to comply. Riots spread throughout the city along with growing reports of new cases of nekrosis.

Xavier greeted Councilman Soros with good news.

"I have received word from Dr. Necropolis that the final batch of Nekrotek is ready to be transported from the Death Factory," said Xavier.

Councilman Soros smiled and said, "I believe it is time that we concluded our business with Manzini."

Together they entered one of the ziggurat's private elevators reserved only for the members of the Supreme Council.

"If that is your wish, I'll see to it immediately," said Xavier.

"Nothing would please me more," said Councilman Soros. "Be sure to see to the inner circle of the Black Nobility once they no longer hold court with Princess Destiny. I don't want them wandering around and stumbling into matters that don't concern them."

"I have some containment cubes where I'm sure they'll feel right at home," said Xavier.

"Makes sure it's somewhere deep down in the bowels of the ziggurat," said Councilman Soros.

"What about General Grindcore?" said Xavier.

The elevator stopped.

"I will let you know when he has outlived his usefulness along with the rest of the Imperial Armada," said Councilman Soros. "Now tell me, what is the status of the daughter of Governor Champagne?"

Councilman Soros exited the elevator.

"Her status is unknown to me," said Xavier. He exited the elevator behind Councilman Soros, and together they entered the Temple of Oblivion from a passageway behind the throne.

"Interesting," said Councilman Soros, "no one in the Occult Bureau has been able to locate any information on her whereabouts?"

"Scarzensky hunts her as we speak," said Xavier.

"The thought has occurred to me," said Councilman Soros, "now that her father is gone perhaps her proper place is amongst the temple prostitutes?"

"If it pleases Oblivion, so be it," said Xavier.

"Indeed," said Councilman Soros.

Xavier walked over to the Jewel of Wisdom and peered deep into the kaleidoscope-like geometry within it as it hovered magically in the middle of the Sigil of the Great Architect of the Universe.

There was a moment of silence.

"The Great Year is complete," said Xavier. "The gateway to the Void will be rising soon."

"And the dawn of a new aeon with it," said Councilman Soros.

"How strange it seems, that we are so close to regaining the lost immortality of our ancestors," said Xavier.

"It has taken us what seems like an eternity to rebuild this temple and with it give birth to an empire that now stretches out to the four corners of all that remains of the Architect's most beloved creation," said Councilman Soros. "All of the Immortal Kingdoms and the Golden Triangle of the Flower Children are now ours."

"One does wonder why our master did not kill him sooner?" said Xavier.

"The ways of Oblivion are not easily understood," said Councilman Soros.

"And yet here we stand before the Jewel of Wisdom," said Xavier, "ready to free our master from his prison. For at that moment, we will look out into the cosmos and fear nothing. Together, we will rise above the heavens as we escape the cruelty of the grave and proclaim ourselves, just like our ancestors that came before us, that we are immortal."

"We will be more than immortal, my faithful servant," said Councilman Soros. "We will be more powerful than the creator of this world."

"What a glorious thought, indeed," said Xavier.

11

FLEUR DE LIS

Officer Whistle Britches peered through the back passenger side window of the Shadow Runner as it pulled into the parking lot of the Fleur De Lis. He couldn't believe the number of people trying to get into the club. There was a line wrapped around the building that looked like it was a mile long and there had to be at least twice as many people loitering around in the parking lot. It seemed that regardless of the riots, and in spite of the quarantine, there were still plenty of people looking to have a good time.

"So, how exactly do you know these pirates?" said Officer Whistle Britches.

Alexis turned the wheel of the Shadow Runner and went down a row of parked cars peppered with club kids.

"Junebug's grandmother, Momma Nymms, was my nana," she said.

"And, you trust him?" said Officer Whistle Britches.

"He's like a brother to me, of course, I trust him," said Alexis. "We might as well be kin."

Alexis parked the Shadow Runner. Everyone exited the vehicle and made their way across the parking lot. As they approached the door, one of the bouncers glanced in their direction.

"Who dat is?" the bouncer half-joked.

Alexis knew who it was.

"What up, Boudreaux?" she said. "How you been?"

Boudreaux smiled.

"I can't complain," he said.

"Don't do no good anyway," said Alexis.

"G'naw, they only make fun of ya if ya do," said Boudreaux.

Alexis giggled and put her hand on her hip.

"Junebug inside?" she said.

Boudreaux made a face like someone who'd seen a sucker.

"Yeah, he's up in there all boo-booed up with Minx," he said.

Boudreaux motioned to the doorman to let Alexis in. The doorman unlatched the security rope. Alexis and 808 walked through it. Boudreaux didn't mind them, but when it came to Officer Whistle Britches, he had an entirely different disposition. Boudreaux looked Officer Whistle Britches up and down like a rodeo clown. He couldn't believe what he was seeing. The calculator watch didn't help. In a gruff and intimidating voice Boudreaux said, "Where you think you're going buster, this ain't no science fair?"

"Buster!" shouted Officer Whistle Britches. He was insulted.

"It's cool, Boudreaux. He's with me," said Alexis. She put her arm around Boudreaux's neck and stuck her tongue out at Officer Whistle Britches. Alexis thought the situation was kinda funny. Officer Whistle Britches was not amused. Boudreaux could see the people still waiting in line were beginning to get impatient. He cocked one eye back and thought about what he was about to do.

"A'ight," said Boudreaux. "I'm gonna make an exception this time 'cause he's with you."

"Thanks, I owe you one," said Alexis. She kissed Boudreaux on the cheek and walked inside the club.

Officer Whistle Britches scurried in behind her. He gave Boudreaux a dirty look.

Boudreaux gave him one back and said, "But make sure you keep him off the dance floor. We gotta reputation to uphold 'round here and it ain't with squares n' tricks!"

Inside the Fleur De Lis, Alexis, 808, and Officer Whistle Britches entered the area surrounding the dance floor. Barre Babies served everyone their drinks. On the wall behind the bar hung a television tuned to WXTZ Channel 13. A wanted poster for Alexis appeared on-screen. The reward was a million credits all paid in Scrilla.

"It's a good thing he let me in. I thought I was about to have to put my hands on him," said Officer Whistle Britches. He tarded-out in front of everyone and started slinging his arms around like he was swimming with his fists clenched.

"Whatever," scoffed Alexis. "Boudreaux would've beat you down."

Nebula, the Bounty Hunter, got up from his bar stool and made his way to the nearest Bit Browser. On its screen, he pressed the icon for the Occult Bureau and connected to their tips hotline. Nebula entered a special numerical command sequence on the browser's keypad. Special Agent Scarzensky appeared on the screen of the Bit Browser.

Alexis, 808, and Officer Whistle Britches walked across the dance floor. On stage, Erotika, the most famous singer in the Black Sun Empire rocked the mic and trillstepped the crowd into a frenzy as she sang her hit song, *It's Expensive,* off her number one hit album entitled, *Braaapp!!!*

"...tha' ringz !!! tha' show'z !!! tha' diamond'z !!! tha' clothez!!! it'z expensive !!! it'z expensive!!!" rang out through the club while Erotika danced with her backup singers, The Freakazoids. The crowd loved it.

Alexis, 808, and Officer Whistle Britches exited the dance floor. 808 walked up the stairs that led to the Velvet Room. Alexis and Officer Whistle Britches checked the booths by the dance floor for Junebug. When 808 got to the top of the stairs, he motioned to Alexis that he'd found him.

"Come on," she said. "Junebug's upstairs."

Junebug was playing cards and carousing with a bunch of fellow pirates, the CBR Kingz. His girlfriend Minx sat quietly in his lap with one arm around his neck. On her hand was a C.L.A.W.

C.L.A.W. stood for Cybernetic, Long-range, Artillery, Weapon.

Minx was a real dime piece.

"Fool, what is up with that fugazi lookin' mess hangin' from around your neck?" said Junebug to Fuckboi.

"What he talkin' 'bout?" said Fuckboi.

Minx couldn't believe how dumb he was.

"Fugazi means it's fake, fool," she said, picking at his ignorance. "Ain'tchu never had no book learning?"

"Hell g'naw, dat fool smokes incense," said Junebug. Everyone around the table except for Fuckboi roared with laughter, for the luster of Junebug's jewelry knew no end.

"Ya'ah regular high-bred gentleman wit' dat fancy talk ain'tcha?" said Fuckboi. The laughter began to subside. Fuckboi tossed in his bet.

Minx giggled when she saw what Fuckboi threw into the pot and said, "I know you just didn't throw some ole worthless dinars on the table?"

Dinars were the old imperial currency before Scrilla. They were still in circulation, but nobody used them anymore. They were too easy to counterfeit. Junebug leaned over the table to see if Minx was for real or just joking.

"Look here, boy, I'm embarrassed for ya," he said. "This here the grown folk's table. You gotta come correct or not come at all, fool. We ain't playin' Ole Maid."

"Ya mean like dat tired heifer ya call ah ole lady?" said Fuckboi.

Junebug blacked out when he heard the insult. He pushed Minx off his lap and flipped the poker table over. Chips, gold coins and the worthless dinars Fuckboi tried to pass off as something worth having flew everywhere. Junebug pulled out his custom-made .45 caliber handgun, the Kingpin.

Blam! Blam! Blam!

Alexis, 808, and Officer Whistle Britches couldn't believe what they'd just seen. Junebug killed Fuckboi.

Minx tried her best to calm him down.

"Walk it off, baby," she said to Junebug. "Walk it off."

Minx sat Junebug down on a couch next to Alexis.

"Who was that?" she said.

"The kinda fool that still thinks the Great Architect of the Universe rings the school bell," said Junebug.

Alexis laughed.

"Junebug, you ain't right," she said.

"Neither is the rest of the world," said Junebug. He looked Officer Whistle Britches up and down like he was ready to kill him too. "Ain'tchu supposed to be dead?"

"It's okay," said Alexis, "This is Officer Whistle Britches. He's not a tattle-tale."

"He'd better not be," said Junebug.

Alexis thought it best to change the subject and steer the conversation in a different direction before Junebug put a hole through Officer Whistle Britches.

"Anyways," she said, "how you been doing?"

"I've been better," said Junebug.

"I heard you've been sick?" said Alexis.

"Minx thinks it's the early stages of nekrosis," said Junebug. "She said I might have picked up a slow-acting form of it smugglin' tryptamine."

"D'jew see a doctor?" said Alexis.

"G'naw, I gotta warrant out for my arrest with the Occult Bureau," said Junebug. "I go in for treatment, the Hive 'el know, and they'll arrest me. That's my third strike. I'd be facin' life down there in one of them containment cubes in the bowels of the ziggurat."

"You could have come to me for help," said Alexis.

"I know," said Junebug. "But, never mind me. Whatchu lookin' for an ole raisin like Junebug for? I ain't seen you in like forever?"

"I need to use your boat," said Alexis.

"For what?" said Junebug.

"We're sneaking into the Death Factory," said Alexis.

"Girl, have you lost your cotton-pickin' mind?" said Junebug.

"No," said Alexis.

"Then what do you want to go in there for?" said Junebug.

"Show 'em the video," Alexis said to 808.

808 opened the video Officer Whistle Britches recorded in his Podcaster and handed his Grimoire to Junebug. One of the Barre Babies from behind the bar walked up and poured the two of them up a drink in a pair of doubled-up styrofoam cups with a Fleur De Lis airbrushed on the side. Junebug pressed play on the screen of the Grimoire.

"That's Viirus," said Minx when she saw him appear on the screen of the Grimoire. "He was with the Occult Bureau before your father's assassination?"

"Yep," said Alexis.

"How'd you get this video?" said Junebug.

"That's Whistle Britches behind the wheel," said Alexis.

"So that's why they had you branded a traitor," said Junebug. "Ya dead ass done seen too much."

"I'm not a traitor," said Officer Whistle Britches in frustration.

Junebug didn't care.

"Channel 13 says you are so you might as well be," he said.

Alexis and Minx looked at the two of them like they needed to get it together.

"The two of you need to focus," said Alexis.

"I am focused!" said Officer Whistle Britches.

Junebug looked back at the Grimoire. The next video on the Grimoire's playlist was the recording from 808's visor of the assassination of Governor Champagne. When Viirus hit the floor after committing suicide Junebug and Minx saw the Nekrobyte run out of the bullet hole in his skull.

"Tell me that wasn't a Nekrobyte," said Minx.

"It was," said Alexis.

"That is so gross," said Minx.

"It makes you wonder," said Junebug, "if Nekrobytes are so deadly, why was Viirus still alive with one that big inside of him?"

"Maybe," said Alexis.

"What else ya got?" said Junebug. He handed 808 back his Grimoire.

"808 stole a vile of Nekron from a medical crate outside the Crystal Ball," said Alexis. "When Professor Proxy tested the Nekron out on one of the rats in his lab, he discovered nanobots inside of the rat that were altering its genetic structure."

"What were they doin' that for?" said Junebug.

"He said it looked like they were grafting a neurotransmitter to the rat's DNA," said Alexis.

"You think the Nekrobytes that were in the Nekron you took in the Golden Triangle and these nanobots are connected somehow?" said Minx.

"I do," said Alexis.

Junebug thought both long and hard about what he'd just seen and heard.

"How you plannin' on gettin' in there?" he said.

"Through a part of the Death Factories sewer system that empties out into the bayou," said Alexis. "Whistle Britches knows where it's at. He used to be a security guard there."

"That true?" said Minx.

"It is," said Officer Whistle Britches.

"That's gonna be a rough ride," said Junebug. "The bayou around the Death Factory smells like a dead dawg, wit two butt-holes, fartin' napalm, so you can only imagine what it's like inside."

"What about General Grindcore?" said Minx. "We can't get to the Infinity unless we go through one of the Armada's checkpoints."

"I'll take care of General Grindcore," said Alexis.

12

CLOVEN HOOF

A loud banging sound startled everyone in the Fleur De Lis. Battle Android DRN-1, codenamed, Assault and Battle Android DRN-2, codenamed, Battery bashed in the emergency exit door at the back of the club with a Cloven Hoof battering ram. Auxiliary and Enforcer Drones swarmed through the opening. Special Agent Scarzensky commanded a second swarm at the front of the building. Minx ran to the balcony and looked over the rail. She couldn't believe her eyes. Boudreaux was in the process of being arrested at the front entrance while Tactical Drones swarmed onto the dance floor.

"It's the Occult Bureau!" said Minx.

Junebug jumped up from where he was seated and looked over the rail for himself. Sho'nuff, every type of drone imaginable was swarming into the club. It was a full-on infestation. The dance floor emptied out in a panic. Junebug ran over to a slot machine by the bar and pulled its handle. A secret underground passageway opened up behind the bar. He went inside along with several of the CBR Kingz and handed O.G. Kush an AK1200 assault rifle from a hidden arsenal.

"Pass that to Minx," said Junebug.

O.G. Kush passed the AK1200 to Minx. Minx armed the AK1200.

"Follow me," she said. Minx turned and disappeared into the

darkness of the underground passageway. Alexis, 808, and Officer Whistle Britches followed behind her.

Battle Android DRN-1, codenamed, Assault and Battle Android DRN-2, codenamed, Battery, led by Nebula, the Bounty Hunter, made their way toward the Velvet Room with Special Agent Scarzensky and a swarm of Enforcer Drones as fast as they could.

"We'll hold 'em off for as long as we can," said O.G. Kush.

Junebug nodded his head in gratitude and exited down the underground passageway. O.G. Kush led the rest of the CBR Kingz over to the balcony to provide some cover fire. One by one they picked off the Enforcer Drones. Nebula opened fire with a Witch Finder crossbow and killed O.G. Kush. Special Agent Scarzensky, along with Battle Android DRN-1, codenamed, Assault and Battle Android DRN-2, codenamed, Battery, killed the rest of the CBR Kingz as though it were child's play.

In the passageway, Alexis clicked the heart-shaped hologram on her keychain. The Shadow Runner powered up and drove in the direction of Alexis' coordinates. In time, the underground passageway came to a stairwell. One by one our heroes raced upward. Once they reached the top, Minx was the first to emerge from the stairwell from behind a door that opened up into a parking garage two blocks over from the Fleur De Lis. Alexis and Officer Whistle Britches exited the stairwell behind her. Junebug upon emerging from the stairwell with 808 by his side, ran for his SUV, the HighRoller. It was powered-up and ready to roll with Minx behind the wheel. Alexis, 808, and Officer Whistle Britches ran for the Shadow Runner as it pulled up beside the HighRoller. Once all of our heroes were inside their respective vehicles, the Shadow Runner and the HighRoller peeled out, leaving skid marked trails full of fire and smoke. Nebula emerged from the stairwell. He could see the two vehicles racing toward the exit of the parking garage. There was no way Nebula could catch them. He aimed the Witch Finder, locked-on to the back of the HighRoller, and fired a tracking device at the back of the vehicle. It landed on the back bumper of the HighRoller just before it exited the parking garage and spun out onto the street.

The Shadow Runner and the HighRoller raced down several city blocks. The red and blue lights of a Stalker ran up alongside them, the

Enforcer Drone inside requested backup. Alexis gripped the steering wheel of the Shadow Runner so hard she was white-knuckled. A Warlock helicopter piloted by a Drone Commander appeared out of nowhere. It hovered down into the road and blocked the on-ramp to the Super Highway in front of the Shadow Runner and HighRoller. Alexis spotted some road construction and accelerated. Road cones were everywhere along with a bunch of heavy equipment. It was a scary little patch of road. The Warlock opened fire on the Shadow Runner.

Alexis wasn't scared.

"Arm weapon systems," she said.

Two machine guns came out of both sides of the front of the Shadow Runner. Several holographic targeting systems covered the windshield. Alexis opened fire. Officer Whistle Britches put his hands over his eyes. They hit the ramp. The Shadow Runner sailed through the air right over the top of the Warlock. Bullets sprayed in every direction. The Shadow Runner landed safely on the Super Highway. Officer Whistle Britches couldn't believe it. The Drone Commander turned the Warlock and chased after them. He flew up behind the Shadow Runner. Two 30mm cannons opened fire from beneath the Warlock. The Shadow Runner swerved to avoid the cannon fire. Alexis' fingernails dug into the bottoms of the palms of her hands. The 30mm cannons of the Warlock destroyed the road around the Shadow Runner. 808 tapped his armrest. A small Blow Torch rocket launcher appeared from beneath the armrest. The front passenger side window of the Shadow Runner descended. 808 locked-on to the Warlock and pulled the trigger on the Blow Torch. A warning signal rang out in the Warlock. The missile from the Blow Torch hit the Warlock.

Ka-Boooom!

The wreckage of the Warlock crashed through a giant billboard advertising Mega Bites Pizza Rolls. Minx swerved to miss the falling debris. 808 was pleased, but there was no time to celebrate. In the rearview mirror, he could see two Enforcer Drones on Blaster motorcycles and a Stalker squadron merging onto the Super Highway from an on-ramp. The Blasters accelerated when they spotted the Shadow Runner and chased after our heroes. They were almost behind them when 808 tapped another button on his armrest. 808's seat folded down and slid backward. The trunk of the Shadow Runner flew open. 808 popped out riding on a tiny motorcycle armed with mini-guns codenamed, the X-orcist. When he hit the ground, 808 dropped two mines and raced between the Blasters. The mines exploded and destroyed both Enforcer Drones in a fiery explosion of mangled metal.

Minx mashed the power pedal of the HighRoller to the floor and pulled up next to the Stalker squadron. Junebug crawled out of the front passenger side window of the HighRoller with an AK1200 in his hands. Faster and faster the HighRoller raced down the Super Highway. Junebug opened fire with the AK1200 and sprayed enough rounds laced with thermite explosives into the Stalkers pursuing the Shadow Runner to stop an Imperial Think Tank. When they exploded, the explosions were so high they could be seen from several city blocks away.

13

DEAD MAN'S CURVE

Near, Dead Man's Curve, General Grindcore saw the Shadow Runner approaching the checkpoint to exit the Super Highway into the bayou. He was going to put an end to Alexis' getaway. A silly little girl, in a silly little car, was not about to get through him. General Grindcore transformed the Imperial Think Tank he was seated in, into a hi-tech, mechanized suit of Bone Crusher armor armed with a hand-held, gamma-ray burst, War Hammer machine gun.

Alexis stopped the Shadow Runner. On the heads-up display on the windshield was a scan of General Grindcore's weapon systems. Alexis knew she had no choice but to go through him. Their escape depended on her. She said she could handle him. Now was the time to step up. In her rearview mirror, Alexis could see the Super Highway beginning to fill with Imperial Think Tanks.

"Get out," said Alexis.

Officer Whistle Britches dove into the Super Highway and fired the DDT in the direction of the approaching Imperial Think Tanks. Alexis slammed the power pedal of the Shadow Runner to the floor. The blast from the DDT flew by the HighRoller and cleared the Super Highway of Imperial Think Tanks. The Shadow Runner raced toward Dead Man's Curve. Alexis was beyond focused. Nothing could stop her now, not even General Grindcore.

Alexis ramped the Shadow Runner into the air.

"I'm going to break every bone in your puny little body!" said General Grindcore. He posted up and fired a huge gamma-ray burst from the War Hammer at the Shadow Runner. The gamma-ray burst missed the Shadow Runner as it transformed into a hi-tech mechanized suit of armor. It surrounded and shielded Alexis. She fell back to the ground. A heart-shaped hologram glittered on her chest plate.

"I don't mind the pain," said Alexis.

General Grindcore pulled the trigger of the War Hammer.

Alexis was fearless. She ran head-on into the gamma-ray burst and blocked it with a Z-shield in the shape of a heart-shaped hologram made with her XOXO. The impact of the blast blew her backward across the ground and caused a loud explosion. Alexis dug her heels deep into the ground. She did not fall, nor falter. When Alexis stopped skidding backward, she sprung from the wall of rubble behind her created by the explosion. Alexis raced toward General Grindcore at an unimaginable speed. A jetpack fired off. Faster and faster she hurtled toward General Grindcore. Together they collided with a punch that hit him in the chest, so hard, that it pulled his legs out from underneath him.

"Ugggh!" groaned General Grindcore. He could feel his chest plate crack upon the impact of Alexis' punch. General Grindcore almost had a heart attack. It became hard for him to breathe. He thought he was going to die. General Grindcore swung back with his right fist. Alexis ducked the punch. It missed. General Grindcore swung again with the left. It connected, landing upside the helmet protecting the head of Alexis. The punch was so brutal that it temporarily blinded her. Alexis saw a flash of white light. Her nose and mouth began to bleed, General Grindcore hit Alexis in the gut with an uppercut. The punch knocked the wind out of her.

"Ughkk!" groaned Alexis. For a moment, she felt like she might puke. With all of her strength, Alexis swung back, bashing General Grindcore in the crack on his chest plate. Over and over again she punched him.

Boooom! Boooom! Boooom!

General Grindcore's armor started to malfunction. It overheated.

His weapon systems misfired. Alexis elbow smashed General Grindcore in the face. He fell into a pile of rubble. Alexis stood tall in a battle ready position. General Grindcore struggled to his feet. In one last futile attempt at victory, he tried in vain to aim the War Hammer at Alexis. In response, she roundhouse kicked him in the face, breaking his jaw. General Grindcore fell to his knees. One of his eyeballs dangled from the socket. Alexis picked up General Grindcore over her head and finished him off with a backbreaker across her knee. His spine snapped.

"Agghhh!" screamed General Grindcore.

Alexis dropped General Grindcore's broken body to the ground.

The battle was over.

14

CONTROLLED SUBSTANCES INC.

Deep within the Death Factory, the name on the door read,
Carlyle Manzini, CEO, Controlled Substances Inc.

"We're fucked!" shouted Manzini at Xavier's face streaming on a monitor in his office. He punched his desk.

"Everything is fine," said Xavier.

"Everything is not fine!" shouted Manzini. WXTZ Channel 13 streamed on a second monitor in his office. They were broadcasting a video of Alexis snapping General Grindcore's spine like a twig to the whole empire. "Did you see what that little bitch of yours just did?"

"Scarzensky is taking care of it," said Xavier.

"He'd better be," said Manzini. "Otherwise, you tell Councilman Soros that our deal is off!"

"There's no turning back now, Manzini," said Xavier.

"Our agreement was that in exchange for backing your little coup and arming the Orphans of Doom with Nekrobytes, I'd never have to worry about a shakedown from the Emissions Guild or bid on a contract before the House of the Black Widow ever again!" said Manzini. "I did my part! I want my money! I want my contracts!"

"Things have changed," said Xavier.

"Things have changed! Things have changed!" shouted Manzini

"Do you know how much money Dr. Necropolis spent modifying those Nekrobytes so that they could hide as hatchlings?"

"Your debts, nor your losses, have ever been of my creation," said Xavier. *"You were compensated for your research and expenses on more than one occasion."*

"I need those contracts!" screamed Manzini like a maniac. "How are they supposed to give them to me if they're all dead?"

"There are greater issues at hand than your contracts," said Xavier.

"You tell that piece of shit that I want my money," said Manzini. There was a hint of desperation in his voice.

"You're being foolish," said Xavier.

"I should have never agreed to allow you to sit on the board of directors," said Manzini. "With that troublesome cunt of yours running around like a wild animal it's only a matter of time before this shit blows up in all of our faces? You know that don't you or are you dumb enough to be thinking with your dick and not with what's between your fucking ears?"

The image of Xavier on the monitor in Manzini's office degraded in picture quality for a moment then began streaming at its maximum bitrate again. Xavier had long since grown tired of Manzini's temper tantrum.

"I told you once already," he said, *"everything is fine."*

"It better be!" screamed Manzini. "Because if it isn't, I'm not going down alone when that worthless cunt of yours comes looking for someone to take the fall for all of this shit you son of a bitch! If I go down, I'm taking Soros and you with me!"

The transmission ended.

Inside the Temple of Oblivion, Xavier was silent, and then he said, "Summon LaReaux."

A Disciple of Oblivion bowed his head in obedience, turned, and walked out of the temple.

Meanwhile, deep down in the Bayou Beignet, near Driftwood Beach, in a patch of trees that could hide almost anything, the Infinity uncloaked. In the distance, Nebula, the Bounty Hunter, watched from a hidden vantage point atop his motorcycle, the Blood Ryder. He opened a communications link with the Occult Bureau. Minx parked the

HighRoller inside the cargo hold of the Infinity. Alexis drove past Minx in a re-transformed Shadow Runner that was beat up beyond belief. 808 was behind her on the X-orcist. Once they were all inside, the loading ramps folded back into the Infinity, and the cargo hold door closed behind them.

Officer Whistle Britches was impressed with the vessel.

"Will you look at this thing," he said.

808 dismounted the X-orcist. The motorcycle transformed into an extra layer of armor and a handheld laser cannon. 808 bound the laser cannon to the back of his new armor.

Junebug exited the front passenger side door of the HighRoller.

"I'll get everything ready," he said. "As soon as the Infinity's warmed up, we'll re-cloak, and get outta here."

While no one was looking Scarzensky's Roach ran out from under the back seat of the Shadow Runner. It hid undetected amongst some of Junebug's tools. The sound of gunfire broke the momentary silence. Something was shooting at 808.

Zap! Zap! Zap!

Alexis ran to investigate. She shook her head with a smirk on her face when she saw what it was that was causing such a commotion. It was a robotic bat shooting a pair of laser beams out of its eyes. They hit 808 right in the butt. Smoke poured off of his rear end. He danced around in pain. The bat squawked like it was proud of itself and landed on the shoulder of Alexis.

"My, you're a sassy little thing aren't you?" she cooed.

808 mean-mugged her.

"Looks like you've made a new friend," joked Minx.

"Where'd you get her?" said Alexis.

"Junebug made her from a couple of old video game systems he had layin' around," said Minx. "You know him? He's always tinkering with something."

Alexis scratched Sassy under the chin. Sassy liked the attention.

"I like her. She's cute," pattered Alexis playfully. "Like ah itty-bitty tiny babies."

In the cockpit of the Infinity, Junebug was doing a systems check. All seemed well. He fired up the ship's engines. A still stupefied Officer Whistle Britches sat down in the co-pilot's chair. He soaked up every single move Junebug made. Deep down inside, he knew all too well that he'd seen a ship just like this one before somewhere. There was no way that a pirate could buy a piece of gear like this all legal and regal without raising a few eyebrows.

"Lemme ask you something," said Officer Whistle Britches.

"Shoot," said Junebug.

"How'd you come into a fine piece of hardware like this?" said Officer Whistle Britches.

Junebug smiled and said, "I stole it from the Occult Bureau."

Back at the checkpoint, Lolita Sanchez and the news cameras of WXTZ Channel 13 were LIVE on the scene. There were battlecruisers, armored personnel carriers, and Support Drones scattered everywhere. A Security Drone walked by with Killer on a leash. Battle Android DRN-1, codenamed, Assault and Battle Android DRN-2, codenamed, Battery secured the perimeter around the news crew.

Lieutenant Blood was the first to see the report from Nebula. Specialist Gutts and Corporal Gore were anxious to see what he'd received. They could tell by the look on his face that it was something good.

"What is it?" said Corporal Gore.

"It's the bounty hunter that led Scarzensky to the girl," said Lieutenant Blood. He walked over to Special Agent Scarzensky.

Two Medical Drones finished loading General Grindcore into an ambulance.

"What now?" said Special Agent Scarzensky.

"The Occult Bureau just got confirmation from Nebula on the girl's location," said Lieutenant Blood. "She's at Driftwood Beach."

"I already know where she is," said Special Agent Scarzensky.

"There's more," said Lieutenant Blood. "I also got a sitrep from the Star Gazer that a missing swarm of hatchlings has been detected sending a transmission from a lab rat at Zohar University."

"Any idea whose lab it is?" said Special Agent Scarzensky.

"The Hive said it was Professor Proxy's," said Lieutenant Blood.

"Governor Champagne's lackey?" said Special Agent Scarzensky.

"The one and only," said Lieutenant Blood.

Special Agent Scarzensky took the tablet from Lieutenant Blood.

"How long have they been transmitting from that location?" he said.

"It's hard to say, there's some interference with the signal," said Lieutenant Blood. "You want us to look into it or do you want us to go after Alexis?"

Special Agent Scarzensky didn't have time to waste on hatchlings.

"I'll talk care of the girl," he said. "The three of you take a swarm of Enforcer Drones and go get those hatchlings."

"What do you want us to do with Professor Proxy?" said Lieutenant Blood.

"If he's there arrest him and let Chancellor Thorn decide his fate," said Special Agent Scarzensky.

Lieutenant Blood didn't like dealing with Xavier.

"You gonna tell him there was a leak, or do you want me to?" said Lieutenant Blood.

"I'll tell him," said Special Agent Scarzensky. "You go get those hatchlings before someone has time to figure out what they are."

15

GOBLIN FARTS

Not too far passed Catfish Junction, in a lagoon watered by Turtlehead Creek, the Infinity approached the tunnels of the sewer system that led into the bowels of Industrial Plant No. 213. The trees that grew up out of the bayou's polluted waters were without a single leaf or piece of moss upon them. They were naked and reached up from the bayou's murky depths like the hands of the dead trying to pull anyone or anything within their reach into the misery that surrounded them. The Death Factory itself filled the entirety of Jekyll Island. There was a gaggle of old administrative buildings that gave it the look of a concentration camp. Industrial smokestacks rose up into the sky and spewed every type of filth imaginable into the air of the city that made the simple act of growing a garden almost impossible in many districts. Anything the nekrotik rain touched died, hence its nickname amongst those that lived in Zohar as the Death Factory.

The smell was awful.

808 wrote something on his Grimoire and handed it to Officer Whistle Britches.

"Smells like goblin farts," said Officer Whistle Britches as he read aloud what 808 had written and he pointed to a cloud of nauseous gas coming from the Death Factory. It settled above the water like a fog.

"That ain't no lie," said Junebug. "That mess has got Zohar smellin' like a dirty diaper, mane."

The Infinity entered into the tunnel of the sewer system underneath the Death Factory. On the main deck, Alexis was by herself. She was standing next to a guardrail. Scarzensky's Roach concealed itself on the rail's underbelly from all prying eyes.

Minx could see something was bothering Alexis.

"Whatcha reading baby?" she said.

"It's a letter my father gave Professor Proxy before he died," said Alexis.

"What's it say?" said Minx.

"It's kinda crazy," said Alexis.

"Try me," said Minx.

"Father wrote," said Alexis, "that he had a spy amongst the Disciples of Oblivion that told him that Mystre initiated Xavier into the highest degree of discipleship, the Keeper of the Infernal Secrets, and that Xavier swore an oath before the Priestess of Oblivion that he would aid her in her quest to free the Spirit of Oblivion from the Void."

"Chancellor Thorn doesn't have that kind of power," said Officer Whistle Britches. "Does he?"

"Growin' up," said Junebug, "Momma Nymms use to read to us the Legends of the Old Wizard Bones all the time 'bout how every million years upon the completion of the Great Year—"

"What's the Great Year?" said Officer Whistle Britches.

"The time it takes for the gateway to the Void to travel from one end of the universe to other," said Junebug. "When it's completed that journey it'll come into perfect alignment with the Sigil of the Great Architect of the Universe. If one of the pure-blooded descendants of the children of Oblivion and Psydonia stands in the center of that sigil, in the Triangle of Manifestation, and places the Jewel of Wisdom into the pommel of the Midnight Sun it'll give the blade of that sword the power to destroy the Sigil of the Great Architect of the Universe and free the Spirit of Oblivion from the Void."

"When's the Day of the Lord?" said Officer Whistle Britches.

"Today," said Junebug.

"I don't understand why Xavier would be involved in such wickedness?" said Alexis.

Minx recognized the naivety.

"You still love him, don't cha?" she said.

"Like cookie dough," said Alexis.

"When they triflin' you can't help but love 'em twice as much," said Minx with a smile on her face.

"Didn't look like his ass was missin' ya too much when he left ya for dead in the hospital and was sellin' his soul," said Junebug.

"Ain't no nobody askin' you, Junebug!" Minx snapped back.

"Woman," said Junebug, "if you holler at me like that one more time I'm gonna throw you overboard."

Minx pulled out a pistol she had hidden and unchambered a bullet. The bullet spun in the air for a second then landed in her hand. Minx tossed the bullet at Junebug.

"Catch!" she said.

Junebug caught the bullet.

"What'd you throw this at me for?" he said.

"Talk to me like that again," said Minx, "and we'll see if your punk ass catches the next one!"

Without warning, Sassy cried out. From the sound of her voice box, everyone knew that something was wrong.

Junebug enhanced the Infinity's radar system.

"What is it?" said Officer Whistle Britches.

Junebug's stomach dropped.

"It's the Occult Bureau," he said while trying not to panic.

"I thought we were cloaked?" said Alexis.

"We are!" said Junebug.

16

PANOPTICON

In the cockpit of a Panopticon aerial attack vehicle, Special Agent Scarzensky armed the targeting system on the monitor in front of him. Battle Android DRN-1, codenamed, Assault and Battle Android DRN-2, codenamed, Battery, assisted Special Agent Scarzensky as his copilots. Special Agent Scarzensky locked-on to the Infinity and blasted it with round after round of cannon fire. Explosions blew the Infinity up against the wall of the tunnel of the Death Factory's sewer system.

Junebug boosted the Infinity's deflector shields. They powered up to full capacity. Junebug reached to his right and clicked a switch labeled *Turrets*. The deck of the Infinity opened up. Two militech railguns capable of producing massive amounts of kinetic energy ascended from the deck below. 808 and Minx ran to their battle stations. Minx armed her turret first. 808 followed her lead and jumped onto one of the turrets beside her. He adjusted his seat. A monitor with a targeting system displayed on its screen appeared in front of him. Once locked and loaded, the turrets 808 and Minx were on raced down a conveyor belt attached to the guardrail of the Infinity.

In hot pursuit of them were a swarm of S.C.A.N.N.E.R.S.

S.C.A.N.N.E.R.S. stood for Sentient, Combat, Aerial, Neural, Network, Enforcement, Robot, Soldier. They were Enforcer Drones that could fly via a mobile jetpack system. In several Hydra battleships, Wetland Drones surrounded the Infinity. They were attempting to box the Infinity in so that Junebug would be forced to slow down and give up because there would be nowhere for him to go.

Minx appeared on the monitor in front of 808.

"Shoot the barrels, fool!" she screamed, so loud, it distorted the audio of her transmission.

808 targeted a barrel of toxic waste floating in front of a Hydra on his monitor. He opened fire. It exploded. The Hydra's targeting computer displayed, *Hull Damage,* then was engulfed in the explosion. The Wetland Drones inside the Hydra crashed head-on into the wall of the tunnel. Over and over again, Minx and 808 picked off each and every enemy, until there were no Hydras and Wetland Drones left to threaten the Infinity.

Nebula, from inside a Head Hunter class dreadnought, could see how well they were doing. He fired several shots at Minx. Lasers flew by on both sides of her and grazed her head. Minx grabbed her burnt hair. It was a close call. Minx opened fire on Nebula with a kinetic burst from her turret and ripped the Head Hunter in half.

808 dismounted his turret. Alexis found herself swarmed and in need of his help. 808 ran below deck into the Infinity's armory. Underneath some of Junebug's tools, there was a weapons chest. 808 opened it. Inside was a high-powered Brain Scrambler sniper rifle. He grabbed it and ran back up to the main deck in time to see Officer Whistle Britches fire the DDT off the back of the Infinity. The shockwave from the explosions caused by the DDT was forcing Scanners to crash land on the deck. It looked like Officer Whistle Britches had everything under control when one slammed right into him.

"Ughhnfff!" groaned Officer Whistle Britches.

He never knew what hit him.

Alexis opened fire with her Enigmas. She shot several Scanners. One crashed on the deck beside her and skidded away. Its jetpack was still in one piece. Alexis ran over to it, picked it up, and put it on. She was about to take off when 808 handed her the Brain Scrambler. Alexis looked at him with a loving smile, armed the boosters on her jetpack, and flew off. Special Agent Scarzensky spotted her. The Panopticon turned. Battle Android DRN-1, codenamed, Assault and Battle Android DRN-2, codenamed, Battery, continued to pummel the Infinity with the Panopticon's laser cannons. Special Agent Scarzensky aimed the Panopticon's missile systems at Alexis and opened fire.

Alexis raised the Brain Scrambler. Inside the scope, she could see that she had Special Agent Scarzensky dead to rites. Alexis fired a round through the protective glass of the Panopticon's cockpit and hit Special Agent Scarzensky right between the eyes. The cockpit exploded as the Panopticon's missiles flew by Alexis. The explosion roasted the flesh off of Special Agent Scarzensky's metallic interior revealing his cybernetic body underneath. He was still alive, yet heavily damaged. The Panopticon raced toward the wall of the tunnel.

"Aiiieeeaahhh!" screamed Special Agent Scarzensky.

The Panopticon hit the wall of the tunnel and exploded into the largest fireball that anyone back on the Infinity had ever seen.

Meanwhile, across the city, beneath the Temple of Oblivion in one of the Occult Bureau's many surveillance rooms deep in the bowels of the ziggurat, Xavier could see what had just happened in the sewer's tunnel thanks to Scarzensky's Roach.

"Imbeciles!" shouted Councilman Soros.

The battle was over.

Councilman Soros stormed out of the surveillance room.

The Surveillance Drones in the surveillance room were unfazed. They continued to monitor the status of the Infinity and its crew.

Xavier exited the surveillance room through a secret passageway behind a vast array of computer monitors. He walked for a while, alone, through a long dark corridor filled with little light. The shadow of a black widow spider with the head and torso of a woman crawled across the wall alongside him.

"What is it that vexes thee?" said Psydonia. "Doest thou still feel the pain from the loss of thy son?"

"I grow tired of Councilman Soros," said Xavier.

"Remember, young disciple," said Psydonia, "people are like skull flowers. Some need no help to grow upright and strong, others struggle, and need guidance along the way, some show promise, yet are lost amongst the weeds, while others perish, and never make it past the seed. Meditate upon these things if you wish to shed your mortal coil and become a Master of the Ancient Electronic Arts. For in unknown pleasures, and in forbidden dreams, you know, that in the darkest shadows that crawl across your wicked, little heart, it is the Spirit of Oblivion that beckons to you. Never forget that once he is reborn, he will not deny you, any desire, of your ancestors, once, immortal flesh."

"All I want is my family back," said Xavier as the promises of Psydonia echoed through his head, and he thought about how much he missed the love of Alexis.

17

HYPERDRIVE

Somewhere beneath the Death Factory, in a darkness that only demons know, Officer Whistle Britches staggered to his feet. Alexis landed on the deck of the Infinity next to him.

"You alright?" she said.

"Yeah," said Officer Whistle Britches, "I just got the wind knocked out of me."

The engine of the Infinity rattled like a lung with tuberculosis.

"That doesn't sound good," said Minx.

In the engine room of the Infinity, a Repair Bot assisted Junebug. He was trying to fix the damage done by the Panopticon.

"Damn it!" yelled Junebug in frustration.

"What is it?" said Minx.

"One of the power cores blew out in the hyperdrive," said Junebug. "The Infinity's going nowhere."

Things were beginning to look hopeless.

"It's only a matter of time before the Occult Bureau sends reinforcements," said Alexis.

Junebug stood up and rubbed the top of his head. On the console in front of him was a full computer readout of every system onboard the Infinity. There was nothing he could do without a replacement core. They were sitting ducks.

"We'll have to use the life rafts and find another way out," said Junebug. He walked up the steps that lead out of the engine room and back out onto the main deck of the Infinity.

Minx followed behind him.

"Junebug use your head. We've got to get this ship repaired," she said. "Think about it. How are we gonna protect ourselves in a couple of life rafts if the tunnels are bound to be crawling with drones soon?"

Junebug knew she was right. He looked around the tunnel for a second and spotted the Head Hunter. It was slowly sinking into the nekrotik ooze that flowed through the tunnel.

"I can take a couple of Repair Bots and try to salvage a core out of that dreadnought before it sinks," he said. "As of right now, that's the only way that I can see that we'll be able to get the engine going and re-cloak."

Minx liked what she heard.

"You sure that will work?" she said.

A wave of uncertainty waltzed across Junebug's face.

"To tell you the truth, I don't even know if it's possible to escape undetected at this point," he said. "I'll go see what I can find. You go arm the probes and see if they can find us a way out of here other than the way we came in."

Junebug turned to leave.

"Be careful," said Minx.

"I will," said Junebug, then he was gone.

Minx turned to Alexis.

"While Junebug is getting that core," she said, "you and 808 go inside, and find whatever it is that you came looking for before the Occult Bureau's reinforcements arrive."

"What about you Whistle Britches?" said Alexis. "You going or staying?"

"I'll stay here and keep a lookout while Minx preps the engine for Junebug," said Officer Whistle Britches. "The basement level entrance into the factory is just up ahead; you can't miss it."

"Take Sassy with you," said Minx. "If anything should happen to the two of you her optics will stream to us your location and what's going on inside."

Back at Zohar University, Lieutenant Blood, Specialist Gutts, and

Corporal Gore pulled up outside the entrance to the building housing the lab of Professor Proxy. A swarm of Enforcer Drones accompanied them.

Inside his lab, Professor Proxy closed the hatch that contained all of Floppy's most vital computerized parts and software programming.

"There, all done," he said to Floppy. Floppy jumped up and licked Professor Proxy on the face as a thank you. Professor Proxy smiled and said, "Well, you're welcome."

The tail-wagging was interrupted by the sound of a monitor popping up in front of them. *Post-implantation Genetic Diagnosis Complete* appeared on its screen.

Mode 7 Graphics Initiated...

Rendering Module...

The vital signs of the lab rat injected with Nekron earlier in the evening began streaming.

"Huh," mumbled Professor Proxy. He scratched his beard. Floppy looked up at him and tilted his head like he was confused. "The graft is a neurotransmitter. But what's it communicating with?"

The nanobots from all over the lab rat's body gathered together in a swarm in the rat's spleen.

"Computer trace signal," said Professor Proxy.

Signal Analysis Initiated...

Imperial Network Relay Authorization Confirmed...

H.I.V.E. Signature Detected...

The tracer found only one place it could be coming from, the Star Gazer, and from there it was sending and receiving encrypted data, to and from, not only every Imperial Think Tank on patrol but to the Hive as well. Professor Proxy found himself, lost, deep in his thoughts, when without warning, the nanobots flooded the lab rat's circulatory system with Nekrotek and hatched into Nekrobytes. The Nekrobytes burst forth from the spleen of the lab rat. Nekrotik tumors began to form throughout its major organs that the Nekrobytes devoured like piranhas.

A single Enforcer Drone raised his leg. He kicked open the door to Professor Proxy's lab. Floppy barked like a wild animal. Professor Proxy threw his hands up in the air. Enforcer Drones surrounded him with the lasers of their Baphomets aimed at his head.

Lieutenant Blood, Specialist Gutts, and Corporal Gore entered the lab. Lieutenant Blood spotted the Nekrobyte transmission on the monitor next to Professor Proxy.

"Well look what we have here," he said. "Seize, everything."

Auxiliary Drones swarmed the lab and started carrying out all of Professor Proxy's files and equipment. His entire lab was being seized down to the last paperclip.

"You can't do that!" shouted Professor Proxy.

Two Enforcer Drones grabbed Professor Proxy by each arm. Specialist Gutts approached him. He gripped the Circuit Breaker in his hand like a baseball bat and bashed Professor Proxy in the middle of his stomach with it. Professor Proxy's knees buckled. He vomited. The two Enforcer Drones holding Professor Proxy began the process of dragging him out of the lab with his intestines burning like they were on fire to an awaiting Imperial Prisoner Transportation Unit. Floppy attacked one of the Enforcer Drones.

"Will somebody, please shut that dog up?" said Corporal Gore.

Specialist Gutts stunned Floppy with his Circuit Breaker and placed him in a cage with a muzzle over his face.

18

MISTRESS LAREAUX

It was dark in Manzini's office. Trixxxy, one of the many escorts Manzini kept in his employ, was sucking on a lollipop. Manzini sprinkled some stardust all over her breasts and then snorted it out of the crack between her tits.

"Why don't we have to take Nekron?" said Trixxxy while twirling her hair. "I mean, how come we don't have to obey Chancellor Thorn and everyone else has to?"

Manzini didn't appreciate her line of questioning.

"You ever tell anybody that, I'll kill ya," he said.

Trixxxy looked at Manzini like he'd lost his mind. Deep down inside, she was scared of him. A deathlike silence surrounded them. Something flickered in Manzini's peripheral vision. The door to his office was open. Bloody brains and skull fragments splattered all over Manzini's face.

Mistress LaReaux appeared from the darkness.

Trixxxy's lifeless body fell to the floor.

"Ah-uh-i-uhhhh!" panicked Manzini.

Mistress LaReaux walked behind Manzini's desk and clicked a button on the keyboard of his computer labeled *Stream*. Xavier appeared on the screen of the monitor on the wall.

"I bailed your dope fiend ass and the piss poor excuse for a company you

call a family business out of trouble," he said, "and you repay me by threatening to blackmail me."

Manzini groveled before the image of Xavier.

"I'm sorry!" he said. "I didn't mean to anger you! I became ungrateful! I forgot myself!"

Mistress LaReaux removed the silencer from her Tombstone revolver.

"I want you to answer me truthfully," said Xavier. *"Don't lie to me and I might let you live. Who switched the Nekron?"*

"Soros paid me to do it," said Manzini.

"Why?" said Xavier.

"I don't know," said Manzini. "He wouldn't tell me."

"Kill him," said Xavier.

"No! No!" Manzini cried like a shook bitch. He shit his pants. It was an appalling spectacle. Mistress LaReaux had no pity. She aimed the Tombstone at the back of his head and blew his brains out all over the monitor on the wall in front of her. Manzini's dead body fell to the floor. Mistress LaReaux took out her Huntress machete and chopped off Manzini's head. She placed it in a hunting pouch, took out a tarot card, and threw it on his lifeless body. The card landed face up revealing that it was Death.

Xavier was pleased.

Mistress LaReaux started to walk away.

"LaReaux," said Xavier. Mistress LaReaux paused long enough to look over her shoulder. *"Bring me, Alexis."*

19

THE LAB OF DR. NECROPOLIS

Bathed in the black light of 808's glow sticks, the butterfly tattoo on the back of Alexis' neck seemed to flutter behind Sassy as her eyes scanned the sewer system of the Death Factory for threats. Alexis had on a new set of armor from the Infinity's armory on the back of which was bound a Skorpion machine gun. Our small band of heroes made their way into the underbelly of the Death Factory. It was crawling with vermin. There was maggotoid slime on the walls and filth teeming with disease. 808 didn't like the looks of any of it, neither did Sassy. They came to a dumping ground where the toxic waste from all the chemicals processed by Controlled Substances Incorporated began its journey and flowed out into the bayou. There was an enormous waste containment door. 808 walked up to a keypad that was on the wall beside it and pulled out his Grimoire and a Stream Ripper from his backpack. He attached one end of the Stream Ripper to the chip reading port of the keypad on the wall and the other end to his Grimoire. 808 opened a key generator app. The screen above the keypad flashed. It rebooted. Some source code scrolled across the screen. Eight numbers appeared on the screen of the Grimoire. 808 typed them into the keypad on the wall, 88914121.

The waste containment door started to open.

"That was quick," said Alexis. It was almost too easy.

Without warning, the waste containment door jammed.

808 was small enough that he could squeeze through the crack in the waste containment door without any problem. Alexis squeezed in behind him, so did Sassy. Once inside, 808 found a freight elevator that took them up to a large staging area filled with rows of barrels of Nekrotek. Sassy scanned each row they passed. She was looking for Manzini's office. Alexis took a deep breath. Her lungs and nostrils burned. Her throat felt raw. The back of her mouth became dry. She covered her face with her hand.

Sassy fluttered into a lab. Alexis and 808 followed behind her. The horrors of man and beast alike that they found inside the lab were indescribable. There was an isolation chamber filled with the bones and rotting flesh of pigs, cows, chickens, and sheep. A swarm of full-grown Nekrobytes devoured the macabre mess. Alexis and 808 stopped to glance at the grotesque scene. Sassy landed on Alexis' shoulder. They explored the chambers together for what seemed to be an eternity, wondering, what kind of depraved individual would do something like this?

808 pulled the skirt of Alexis. Once he had her attention, he motioned to an isolation chamber housing a giant, half-mutant, half-robot, monstrosity, labeled, *T.O.R.M.E.N.T.*

T.O.R.M.E.N.T. stood for Technotronic, Operations, Reconnaissance, Mutant, Enforcement, Network, Tracer. With a fang-filled gash of a mouth riddled with jagged teeth, his flesh was mangled with metal and stitched back together with the most designer cryogenically enhanced sutures that Alexis had ever seen. It was as if someone tore him to pieces and then put him back together again, with every step along the way another experiment in a new unspeakable horror, more insane and filled with madness, than the last. On both sides of him were row after row of deactivated semi-cybernetic, half-man, half-machine, zombie militants, individually numbered with a unique serial number and labeled, *Psyborg*. An odor of decay hung in the air of the laboratory like a rotting corpse. Flies began to circle. Alexis swatted a few of them back.

Sassy leapt from her shoulder and fluttered out of the lab.

"I don't like the look of this place," said Alexis to 808. She gave the isolation chamber one last long and graven look. Torment was revolting. At the end of the room, along the wall, once one passed a dozen or so open crates filled with an experimental drug labeled, *Halcyon 1138*, there was a huge mainframe supercomputer. On both sides of it were these sexless mutant creatures, very different from what they had just seen in the chambers housing the Psyborgs. The mutants were labeled, *Goyum*. The Goyum were segregated from one another to ensure that they were isolated and all alone. Their eyes were solid black like they had no souls and their skin was a pale white, like milk.

808 ran to the mainframe. When he got to the mainframe's command console, he hooked up his Stream Ripper to an open data port on the console and attached the other end to his Grimoire.

Boot...

Run xkcd...

A folder labeled, *Nekrogenetics*, appeared on the screen of the monitor on the mainframe. 808 clicked it. Inside the folder were several video files. 808 clicked one. A pregnant woman that worked in the tryptamine mines in the Golden Triangle appeared on the screen of the monitor. The video was vivid and weird, like a drug-induced hallucination that someone had slipped into a dream. Her vital signs showed that her circulatory system contained the same nanobots that were present in the vial of Nekron they'd left with Professor Proxy. The eyes of Alexis widened in horror. The nanobots in the circulatory system of the pregnant woman swarmed together inside her spleen. Once inside, the nanobots released large doses of Nekrotek. When her spleen was full of the mutagen, the nanobots hatched into Nekrobytes and burst forth from the woman's spleen and back out into the circulatory system of not only her but of her unborn child.

The pregnant woman screamed like a gutted beast as an emaciated creature that had once been her child tore through her belly with a Nekrobyte attached to its brainstem like a parasite. The pregnant woman went into shock and passed away while foaming at the mouth, with her eyes, rolled into the back of her head. The child was a humanoid looking mutant, just like the ones with pale milky-white skin and solid black eyes on either side of the mainframe, only this one was smaller. It was born into a form of sub-human misery. Goyum were a new genotype that was neither male nor female. It did not have any genitalia or reproductive organs of any kind. The area where a penis or a vagina would normally be present, instead, was a smooth area of flesh resembling that of a plastic toy doll. Only one hole was present for the excretion of all bodily waste including urine. No nipples were present for breastfeeding. Its existence was an insult to the natural order of what remained of the Gardens of Eternity. It was the poster child for devolution, the denigration of a species, degeneration.

Alexis stared at the mutant Goyum in the isolation chambers next to the mainframe.

"Those things are humans, 808," she said in a state of utter disbelief.

"*Goyum, test subject, number, 1307,*" said Dr. Necropolis, standing before the husk of the pregnant woman. "*When the patient is not with child, those exposed will degenerate into a state of mindlessness. Soon, their major organs will begin to fail, blindness in most cases will occur. Within fifteen to twenty minutes their metamorphoses will be complete, leaving them in a state of utter decay. At this stage, the Nekrobytes will devour the host organism and leave nothing but the husk of a rotting carcass.*"

"This is why Nekron made me sick. It doesn't cure or help prevent nekrosis. It's a preservative used to keep Nekrobytes alive," said Alexis. "The nanobots that Professor Proxy found in the vial of Nekron you gave him, they're nekrobiotic hatchlings disguised as nanobots."

Upon hearing this, 808 started to download copies of the video files onto the drive in his Grimoire.

Alexis took control of the console and scrolled through the video files on the mainframe. She came to one labeled, *Psyborg Corps Beta Test*. She clicked on it. General Grindcore, Councilman Soros, Manzini, and Xavier appeared on the screen of the monitor on the mainframe. Dr. Necropolis demonstrated to the four of them how a Nekrobyte could take control of the dead body of a mercenary by attaching itself in a parasitic fashion to the brainstem of the dead mercenary. The Hive controlled the Nekrobytes via nanite MindBender central processing units similar to the ones found in the Occult Bureau's drones. The MindBenders communicated over the wireless network relays in the Pitch Shifters equipped to Imperial Think Tanks. They gave the Hive full control of the movements of the dead mercenaries and the hatchlings inside of them. Dr. Necropolis modified the bodies of several dead mercenaries and demonstrated their use for combat purposes unfit for the living. Little by little the deactivated semi-cybernetic, half-man, half-machine, zombie militants, came to life.

Everything that had happened to Alexis, the miscarriage, 808's birth defects, the pressure to pass Supreme Council Resolution 33, the forced inoculations, the attack on the Crystal Ball, and the murder of her father, it was all beginning to make sense.

"The nanobots are marking the infected," said Alexis as she gazed into the screen of the monitor on the mainframe, "because it makes them easy to track and catalog. Viirus was under the control of the Hive. That's why we saw the Nekrobyte crawl out of his skull. He was a puppet. They're devolving people, 808. They're killing us off one by one with a nekrobiotic that doesn't even work. General Grindcore, Dr. Necropolis, Councilman Soros, Manzini, and Xavier they all know that exposure to Nekron will alter the genetic structure of whoever takes it. Father was right."

20

PSYBORG CORPS

808 spotted Scarzensky's Roach running down the side of the mainframe. It scurried across the floor. 808 followed the roach across the room until it ran underneath a locked door. The door flew open. Dr. Necropolis was standing behind it with several Psyborgs by his side.

"Kill them!" he screamed.

Alexis grabbed the Skorpion machine gun bound the back of her armor, armed it, and opened fire.

Sassy heard the commotion. She flew back in the direction of the lab as fast as she could. When Sassy arrived at the door to the lab, she discovered that it was locked. Sassy felt a tiny zap. Something shot her. Sassy looked down. On the floor below stood Scarzensky's Roach. Sassy swooped down and grabbed the roach in her tiny mouth and chomped it to death. With each bite, tattered wings and broken legs made of metal fell to the floor underneath her. When Sassy finished, she swooped back over to the door to the lab. On a monitor on the control panel, she could see the small group of Psyborgs armed with Violator machine guns opening fire on Alexis and 808. Sassy tried to override the control panel with an EMP signal from her radar. It didn't work. She'd have to find another way back in. Sassy flew away.

808 dove for cover. From behind a crate of Halcyon 1138, he opened

fire with the X-orcist. The blast blew off an arm of one of the Psyborgs. It severed it at the shoulder, causing the Psyborg to lean over to one side, and strike the vilest of postures. 808 wasn't safe for very long. Dr. Necropolis swung a Corpse Grinder chainsaw at him. 808 ducked, and it busted open one of the isolation chambers. Nekrotik goo poured out everywhere.

Psyborgs surrounded Alexis. She pulled the trigger on the Skorpion in her hands. It jammed. Alexis dropped it and pulled out her Enigmas. She opened fire. Body parts flew everywhere. Alexis jumped over an operating table, and grabbed a modified Wig Splitter bone saw. The Psyborgs continued their chase. Alexis activated the Wig Splitter and ran toward them like a possessed woman. She decapitated two and disemboweled a third, the lab filled with the sound of meat ripping and tearing from the bodies of the Psyborgs. Their entrails spewed everywhere as their bowels fell on the floor before them. The mangled corpses of Psyborgs heaped at the feet of Alexis. Nekrobytes poured out of their skulls.

808 was distracted by all the chaos and his concern for his mother. Dr. Necropolis smacked him with the Corpse Grinder. The blow sent 808 flying across the lab and into the monitor on the mainframe. Bolts of electricity, amidst an explosion of flames, sent a paralytic surge coursing throughout 808's body. His nervous system scrambled. Sparks flew everywhere. 808's entire body shook violently then hit the floor, lifeless.

Dr. Necropolis attacked Alexis. He knocked the Wig Splitter out of her hands and was trying to chop her in half with the Corpse Grinder. Backward she ran dodging his every attack. Dr. Necropolis chopped up everything around him with every missed attempt. Alexis slipped on some nekrotik goo. It was all over the floor around her. Alexis swept the leg of Dr. Necropolis. He fell to the floor with Alexis and lost his grip on the Corpse Grinder. Alexis struggled to scramble to her feet. The floor was as slick as snot. Dr. Necropolis tackled Alexis before she was upright. Alexis hit the back of her head on the floor on her way down. She was flat on her back. Dr. Necropolis crawled on top of Alexis. He reached beside her and picked up the Corpse Grinder. Alexis shook her head. The lab was spinning. She looked over to her right side and saw a group of frayed wires that had come loose from one of the damaged isolation chambers. Dr. Necropolis raised the Corpse Grinder over his head and was about to grind Alexis' face into a mushy pulp. Alexis reached out and grabbed one of the massive frayed wires by its protective coating and plunged its exposed wiring into the side of Dr. Necropolis.

"Ahhhhhhhh!" screamed Dr. Necropolis. He dropped the Corpse Grinder to the floor. Alexis shoved the lifeless body of Dr. Necropolis from atop her. She got up off the floor and ran over to 808. He was lying on the floor in front of the mainframe like a broken toy.

Alexis cradled 808 in her arms.

"Don't die on me 808!" she shouted. "Don't you dare die!"

"Momma!" screamed 808, in the gasp of one last final breath as deep as death from his electronic voice box. He powered down.

"808! Wake up! 808! No! No! Please, don't take my baby boy from me!" cried Alexis, in a place where smiles go to die. Mistress LaReaux snuck up and struck her from behind with the butt of her Tombstone. Alexis collapsed to the floor.

Mistress LaReaux fired a round into the head of 808. Smoke poured from the hole. Dr. Necropolis crawled to his feet.

He was still alive.

21

DETENTION LEVEL 213

The Imperial Prisoner Transportation Unit rattled and echoed throughout the subterranean compound as it entered the ziggurat. The hum of the engines of the Imperial Think Tanks around it was deafening. Professor Proxy's situation depressed him, yet he was better off inside the transport than in his lab. WXTZ Channel 13 broadcast the riots spreading throughout Zohar University LIVE after the fall of the House of the Black Widow. Johnny Lyes said it was a peaceful student gathering in support of Supreme Council Resolution 33.

The convoy came to a stop.

The door to the Imperial Prisoner Transportation Unit opened. Professor Proxy was forced out and nudged along with the threat of being hit again with a Circuit Breaker. Floppy struggled to get the muzzle off of his face while the Support Drones around him unloaded all of Professor Proxy's lab equipment.

"I've gotta go to the temple and see Chancellor Thorn," said Lieutenant Blood. "I just got an update from one of the Medical Drones with General Grindcore. His situation doesn't look good."

"What'd the drone say?" asked Corporal Gore.

"It looks like the little bitch severed his spinal cord," said Lieutenant Blood.

"Ouch!" cringed Specialist Gutts.

"The two of you finish processing Professor Proxy and meet-up with me at Hangar 18," said Lieutenant Blood.

Professor Proxy was shackled to a chain gang by a Containment Drone. A centurion in the Order of the Trapezoid cracked a laser whip, and the prisoners shackled to Professor Proxy began to march in a single file line. When they arrived at Detention Level 213, Professor Proxy found himself in the Pit, one of the Occult Bureau's most dangerous cell blocks deep within the ziggurat's catacombs. Two Containment Drones placed Professor Proxy in a containment cube of his own, where he was unshackled, and imprisoned behind a security shield. Once they saw Professor Proxy was processed and secure, Specialist Gutts and Corporal Gore exited the Pit and entered a personnel elevator that would take them to the level housing Hangar 18.

In the selfsame moment, one of the elite centurions in Princess Destiny's honor guard brought it to her attention that the Occult Bureau had detained Professor Proxy at the Imperial Armada's request. She was shocked at the news and demanded to see him at once. All of the drones and mercenaries in the Occult Bureau and Imperial Armada stood at attention when Princess Destiny arrived in the Pit. She approached the containment cube housing Professor Proxy. Princess Destiny had known him all her life. He was a humble man that had done his best to serve the Black Sun Empire and its citizens in all of his endeavors. All of his patents, inventions, his gained wisdom over the years of his life, had been in the pursuit of one goal, to restore the Gardens of Eternity to their former glory. But now, Professor Proxy found himself in the Pit, locked away like a common criminal, in a horrible place where a man's mind can only wander for so long before it turns inward on itself and goes bonkers.

The security shield of the containment cube powered down. Princess Destiny entered the cube, followed by her honor guard.

"Leave us," she said. Her honor guard obeyed. They left the containment cube and posted up at its entrance along with Maximillion, her robotic black panther.

Professor Proxy was glad to see her.

"Your Highness," he said.

"How are you?" said Princess Destiny.

"I've been better," he said.

"What are the charges against you?" said Princess Destiny.

"I don't know," said Professor Proxy. "No one has told me. All I know is that my troubles started when Alexis brought me a vile of Nekron that contained a swarm of nekrobiotik hatchlings disguised as nanobots within it. I know this without a shadow of a doubt because I injected the Nekron into one of my lab rats at Zohar University. When I ran an analysis on the hatchlings, I discovered that they were removing a piece of the lab rat's DNA and replacing it with a neurotransmitter unlike anything that I'd ever seen before. This neurotransmitter was capable of sending a two-way signal to and from the Star Gazer. This signal was then rerouted and sent to the Hive. It's how I believe the mercenaries were alerted to the fact that I was in possession of them."

"And, what was this signal used for?" said Princess Destiny.

"My best guess is that the neurotransmitter is a tracking device of some sort," said Professor Proxy. "When I traced the signal paths of the Star Gazer the ship wasn't only communicating with the Hive. The Star Gazer was also communicating with the wireless network relays in the Pitch Shifters equipped to the Imperial Think Tanks out on patrol, and they appeared to be transmitting a key code to the hatchlings that allowed them to unlock and hatch into Nekrobytes once they swarmed together inside the spleen of the rat."

"Were they like the ones you found in the blood samples of Alexis before she miscarried?" said Princess Destiny.

"How did you find out about that?" said Professor Proxy. "Did Governor Champagne and Alexis tell you about 808?"

"What about 808?" said Princess Destiny.

"I, uh," mumbled Professor Proxy. He was at a loss for words.

"I'm going to ask you this again, Professor Proxy, and don't you dare lie to me," said Princess Destiny. "Were these Nekrobytes like the ones you found in the blood samples of Alexis before she miscarried her child?"

There was an awkward silence between Princess Destiny and Professor Proxy before he spoke.

"Yes, ma'am," he said.

"What became of them?" said Princess Destiny.

"The mercenaries that raided my lab seized them," said Professor Proxy.

"Where did Alexis get the Nekron from?" said Princess Destiny.

"Outside of the Crystal Ball," said Professor Proxy. "She also has a video of Special Agent Scarzensky and Viirus together before Governor Champagne's assassination proving that she had nothing to do with it."

"Xavier's bodyguard?" said Princess Destiny.

"In all his ugly glory," said Professor Proxy. "The video was recorded by Officer Whistle Britches."

"The dead officer on duty at the Crystal Ball this evening?" said Princess Destiny.

"Yes ma'am," said Professor Proxy, "he's still alive and was with Alexis when she came by my lab earlier thing evening."

"Where is she now?" said Princess Destiny.

"The last time I heard from her she was attempting to make contact with some old pirate friends of hers," said Professor Proxy.

"Whatever for?" said Princess Destiny.

"She wanted them to smuggle her into the Death Factory," said Professor Proxy.

"Has she gone insane?" said Princess Destiny.

"No, Your Highness," said Professor Proxy. "Alexis wanted to gain access to Controlled Substances Incorporated's mainframe to see what Manzini was up to."

Princess Destiny worried about her friend. Why would Alexis do something so foolish and not come to her first?

"I will do my best to see that you are released," said Princess Destiny. She exited the containment cube.

Professor Proxy knew the kind of danger that awaited her.

"Be careful, Your Highness," he said.

Above them, in the Temple of Oblivion, Xavier was bathed in the light of the Jewel of Wisdom. Alone he stood before the Supreme Council.

"Has the Star Gazer been readied?" said Councilman Soros.

"Dr. Necropolis is taking care of the matter as we speak," said Xavier.

"And, what of Manzini?" said Councilman Soros.

"I had Mistress LaReaux see to him," said Xavier.

"Silence General Grindcore as well," said Councilman Soros.

"What about the mercenaries under his command?" said Xavier.

"We have plenty of drones in the streets," said Councilman Soros. "I see no reason to keep them around any longer."

"As soon as I leave here," said Xavier, "I'll see to it that the hatchlings inside of them are activated."

"Good," said Councilman Soros. "What is the status of the daughter of Governor Champagne?"

"She's dead," said Xavier.

"And her friends?" said Councilman Soros.

"They too, are without the breath of life," said Xavier. "I had the tunnels underneath the Death Factory flooded with Nekrotek before it was destroyed."

"Excellent, excellent," said Councilman Soros. "You have done well my boy. Oblivion would be pleased."

"All I do, I do to bring glory to his name," said Xavier.

"So say we all," said Councilman Soros with a smile.

22

CHARM BRACELETS

Mistress LaReaux marched Alexis through the Death Factory. Charm Bracelets shackled her wrists. Alexis had a massive headache. The knot on the back of her head was throbbing so bad it felt like that at any moment it would explode. Sassy was above them in the factory's ductwork. She was forced to crawl along on her belly because the ductwork was too small to fly in. From her vantage point, Sassy could see through the vents in the ductwork that Demolition Drones were everywhere. There were too many of them for her to take on by herself. Mistress LaReaux and Alexis came to an exit that led into a staging area of the Death Factory known as the Boneyard. Alexis shielded her eyes from a dusty whirlwind stirred up by a landing Phantom Lord aerial transport ship. Two Scanners escorted Mistress LaReaux and Alexis onboard. On either side of the craft, Drone Commanders piloting Warlock helicopters sat prepared to escort the Phantom Lord to the ziggurat. The Demolition Drones orders were to destroy the Death Factory. Sassy could see all of this as she peered through the last vent she came to that overlooked the Boneyard.

Dr. Necropolis, with several Psyborgs by his side for bodyguards, was busy overseeing a swarm of HazMat Drones. The HazMat Drones were instructed to begin loading barrels of Nekrotek into the cargo holds of several idling Imperial Waste Management Transports. Inside the Phantom Lord, there was a holding cell. One Scanner placed Alexis inside the cell, the other locked her Charm Bracelets to a chain connected to the floor of the Phantom Lord. Medical Drones secured the carcass of Torment. When the HazMat Drones finished loading the last barrels of Nekrotek into the cargo holds of the Imperial Waste Management Transports their cargo hold doors were folded up and locked behind them.

The Phantom Lord started to take off.

Sassy shot two laser beams from her eyes and blasted the vent she was behind off its hinges. She jumped out and flew off in pursuit of the Phantom Lord. Back on the Infinity, Minx received a transmission from Sassy that the Death Factory was about to be reduced to rubble.

"What is it?" said Officer Whistle Britches. He could see the worried look plastered all over Minx's face.

"It's Sassy," said Minx. "The Occult Bureau arrested Alexis. There's Demolition Drones everywhere. They're going to destroy the Death Factory."

"What about 808?" said Officer Whistle Britches.

"I don't see him," said Minx. "We've gotta get Junebug and get out of here."

Meanwhile, out on the Head Hunter, Junebug pulled hard on one of the power cores that powered its engine.

"Ugghh!" he groaned. It wouldn't budge. The socket stripped. Junebug tossed the ratchet he'd crafted for just such an occasion back into his toolbox at the entrance to the engine room as he walked out onto the main deck of the Head Hunter. Minx's face appeared on the screen of his communicator. Junebug swiped the screen with his thumb and accepted her communications request. A video of Minx started streaming.

"I was just about to call you," said Junebug.

"Alexis got arrested," said Minx.

"What? How?" said Junebug.

"I don't know," said Minx. "Sassy just sent me a video of some Scanners leading her onto one of the Occult Bureau's aerial transport ships. There were Demolition Drones everywhere. We've got to get out of here before they blow this place sky high."

"I just stripped the socket of a power core I found," said Junebug.

"I'm gonna need an extra pair of hands to pry it loose. Other than that, I've got all the components I need to get us out of here."

"I'll be there in a second," said Minx.

Junebug ended the transmission and walked over to the guardrail. Nothing but junk surrounded the Head Hunter, some of which, already found itself covered in maggotoids. They were sinking their fangs into some Nekrotek covering several damaged Wetland Drones. The maggotoids devoured the Nekrotek until the last drop was sucked dry. They turned neon purple and started glowing. Junebug turned to look in the direction of the Infinity to see how far away Minx was. He coughed. There was an eerie quiet in the tunnel that he hadn't noticed before. It was spooky. Everything was silent except for the hypnotic hum of the Infinity's Repair Bots being used to stabilize the Head Hunter and keep it from sinking. Junebug turned back toward the engine room. He wiped his hands on his smuggler's vest and looked up. His stomach dropped. Nebula was standing in front of him with his Witch Finder crossbow aimed right between Junebug's eyes.

"Break yo'self," said Nebula, with a sheepish grin on his face.

Junebug felt like a fool. He'd left his gun lying on top of his toolbox.

"It ain't gotta be like this, mane," said Junebug. "Whatever the Occult Bureau is payin' ya, I'll double it."

Nebula thought Junebug was full of shit.

"You ain't got that kinda scrilla fool," he said. "Bess get tuh steppin'."

"My girl's got it," said Junebug. "We gotta whole chest full of gold back on the Infinity."

Nebula thought for a moment.

"We'll see," he said.

Nebula shoved Junebug. He stumbled a little bit and started to stagger off. Nebula was about to take Junebug below deck when he heard the sound of a gun cocking.

"Drop it," said Minx.

Minx pressed the pistol she was holding up against the back of Nebula's head. The gun's metal was cold. Nebula dropped the Witch Finder. Minx kicked it away. She was off-balance. Nebula turned and elbowed Minx in the face. The pistol in her hand misfired. Nebula kicked Minx into the wreckage of a damaged Hydra next to the Head Hunter. She hit the wreckage and lost her grip on the pistol in her hand. It slipped off the side of the ship and into the ooze.

Junebug scrambled for his toolbox. He grabbed his gun. Nebula rushed Junebug and tackled him to the deck of the Head Hunter. The two of them wrestled with one another. Nebula did his best to pry the gun from Junebug's hands. Junebug, in desperation, squeezed off several rounds into the air.

Blam! Blam! Blam!

Nebula punched Junebug in the face. Junebug's nose started bleeding. He slapped Nebula across the face with the gun in his hand. Nebula's body collapsed to the deck of the Head Hunter. Junebug rolled over. Nebula stood up. Junebug was still laid out on the deck. Nebula stomped Junebug's hand. The gun he was holding came loose. Nebula kicked it across the deck. Junebug blinked his eyes and tried to focus on where Nebula was standing. He crawled to his knees and bum-rushed Nebula. Nebula didn't have the strength to fend off the attack. Junebug tackled him to the deck of the Head Hunter. Nebula struggled to get out from underneath Junebug. He squirmed like a maggotoid. Junebug punched Nebula in the face over and over again. Nebula clicked a button on his utility belt. A ripple of paralyzing energy flowed throughout the armor he had on.

"Ugghnh," groaned Junebug. He slumped from atop Nebula. Nebula staggered to his feet. Junebug didn't move on the deck of the Head Hunter. He was in a state of temporary paralysis. Nebula spit out several teeth from his mouth. He looked down. Blood covered the front of his armor. Nebula stumbled forward and wiped his chin. A hidden knife came out from underneath the sleeve of his armor. Nebula was about to gut Junebug.

Out of nowhere, Minx blind-sided Nebula and hit him with a broken piece of railing. The knife he was holding flew from his hand. Nebula collapsed in pain on the deck of the Head Hunter. He looked over and saw his crossbow was on the deck beside him. Nebula reached out and grabbed it. He rolled over and pointed the Witchfinder at Minx. She knew she was dead. Nebula stood up and was about to pull the trigger when without warning, he let out a blood-curdling scream and was blown backward into the nekrotik ooze flowing through the sewer system, "Aggaaaahh!"

Minx couldn't believe her eyes. Neither could Junebug.

Officer Whistle Britches was standing on the deck of the Head Hunter in a modified ExoSuit equipped with Bionic Legs that he'd synced with his Gravity Boots.

"I see you've been playing in the armory while I was gone," joked Minx.

"I heard the shots and came running," said Officer Whistle Britches.

"I've never been so glad to see the police in all my life," said Junebug. He put his hand on Officer Whistle Britches shoulder. "Come on, let's get that power core and get out of here."

23

X-ORCIST

Back in the lab of Dr. Necropolis, 808 lay lifeless.

Cerebral Hemorrhage Minimized…

Biomechanical Feedback Restored…

Build 13.1.3 Back Online…

Extracting…

Restoring Previous Version…

Project 808.1.2.1.

Installation Complete…

X-orcist Initiated...

These were the programming commands that were displayed on the internal heads-up display on 808's visor as his vision came back into focus. He shook his head. The brain zaps were awful. 808 staggered to his feet. He panicked. Alexis was gone. The tracking device in her necklace was having trouble communicating with 808's internal tracking system. She was getting too far out of range. 808 knew he had to hurry. If he didn't, he would lose the signal and never be able to find her.

808 bent over, grabbed the X-orcist's handheld laser cannon laying on the floor next to him, and ran across the lab. An explosion shook the Death Factory. The ceiling of the lab collapsed in front of him. Rubble

blocked his path back to the Infinity. 808 turned and ran through the door that Dr. Necropolis had been hiding behind. He followed a long dark corridor into the refinement facility of the Death Factory. The refinement of an almost infinite amount of Nekrotek took place before his electronic eyes. Vat after vat stretched on for what seemed forever in every direction. Some were boiling over. The noise was overwhelming.

808 raced down some scaffolding. He was half-way down when another explosion rocked the Death Factory. A vat of unrefined Nekrotek filled with mixing agents tumped over and splashed everywhere. The toxic purple goo began the process of eating away at parts of the scaffolding. A little dripped onto 808's armor. It sent a stinging pain throughout his whole central nervous system. The smell of it was awful. 808 looked up and could see it dripping down in tiny droplets from the scaffolding above him. He knew he had to get out of there and quick. 808 continued down the scaffolding. Droplets of unrefined Nekrotek continued to dribble onto the guardrail beside him.

808 hit the bottom floor running. The explosions in the Death Factory became more frequent all around him. 808 spotted the facilities waste containment door. He approached the keypad on the wall and typed 88914121. The waste containment door unlocked. It slid open. 808 entered the Boneyard.

808's armor transformed into the X-orcist. He revved its engines up and left a blazing trail of smoke and fire behind him. 808 hit the Turbo button on the controls of the X-orcist and raced across the bridge that connected Jekyll Island with the Port of Zohar. Sentinel Drones from the watchtowers between the X-orcist and the security fence of the Death Factory aimed their Baphomets at 808. Their lasers did nothing but break up the ground around the X-orcist. Cluster munitions rained down all around 808. The Sentinel Drones weapons systems couldn't lock-on to the X-orcist. The bike was moving too fast. 808 ramped the X-orcist, hurtled into the sky, and flipped end over end over the security fence. When the X-orcist landed, 808 gripped the handlebars of the X-orcist as though his life depended on it. It took all of his strength to maintain control of the bike. When 808 looked behind him, he could see the Death Factory imploding in on itself. The entire sky lit up like it was the end of the world. A giant sinkhole in the bayou swallowed up the bridge, the watchtowers, and all the Sentinel Drones.

808 turned forward.

In the distance, he could see the Phantom Lord flying through the sky in front of him. By this time, the Infinity had exited the sewer system and was in the process of docking against a shore far away from the Death Factory. Minx and Officer Whistle Britches were standing on its deck. The Death Factory could be seen sinking in the distance.

"I hope 808 wasn't in there," said Minx.

"Me too," said Officer Whistle Britches.

Junebug exited the cockpit of the Infinity during the final explosions. He too hoped that 808 had made it out of the Death Factory alive. Junebug walked below deck. Minx and Officer Whistle Britches followed him into the cargo hold. Junebug opened the cargo hold door and activated the loading ramps. He jumped behind the wheel of the HighRoller and powered-up the engine. Minx called shotgun. Officer Whistle Britches climbed in the backseat. Junebug mashed the power pedal of the HighRoller to the floor. The HighRoller peeled out of the Infinity and onto a small dirt road running through the bayou. It wasn't long until they came to a paved frontage road that ran parallel to the Super Highway. 808 passed in front of the High Roller on the back of the X-orcist. Everyone in the HighRoller was relieved to see that he was alive. The High Roller turned down the frontage road and merged onto the Super Highway behind 808. The display of the onboard navigational computer in the HighRoller started beeping.

"Sassy's still tracking Alexis," said Minx. "They're heading toward the ziggurat."

Meanwhile, outside the Temple of Oblivion, the Disciples of Oblivion were busy cleansing the Altar of the Sleeping Virgin used to sacrifice one of the temple's prostitutes earlier in the evening. Inside, Princess Destiny paced back and forth. Her honor guard was silent. Xavier entered the temple. Princess Destiny rushed toward him.

"Chancellor Thorn, I must insist you release Professor Proxy from his containment cube at once!" she said.

Xavier had no idea what she was talking about, yet still, he was in no mood to hear her bitch.

"You are the first person to bring it to my attention that Professor Proxy is in the Occult Bureau's custody," he said. "What has he done?"

"You know full well why he is here," said Princess Destiny. "Don't you dare play stupid with me!"

"I'd watch your tone when speaking to me," said Xavier.

"I know that it is you, Xavier Thorn, that is behind the current crisis we face," said Princess Destiny. "It is you that has brought this plague upon all of our houses."

Xavier had reached the last reserves of his patience.

"And what is it that you think you know?" he said.

"You have been hiding Nekrobytes disguised as nanobots in the Nekron being administered to our people," said Princess Destiny.

"Seize her," said Xavier. Princess Destiny's honor guard surrounded her. There was nowhere to run. Two centurions broke rank and grabbed each of her arms at the same time that an Enforcer Drone hit Maximillion with a Circuit Breaker and two centurions began the process of chaining him to the Throne of Oblivion. The end was near. Princess Destiny struggled to elude the grasp of the centurions but was too weak to get away. Xavier could see the terror written all over her face. He grinned. "It seems there is no honor left in your honor guard."

Princess Destiny was not amused.

"Whatever it is you're planning," she said, "I promise you it will never succeed, nor come to see the light of day."

"You have no idea how many of your subjects are already dead," said Xavier.

"I'll have you executed for treason!" screamed Princess Destiny.

Her threats fell on deaf ears.

"My dear, sweet Destiny," said Xavier as he looked deep into her eyes and placed his hands on the sides of her face like she was a child. "I am going to take Alexis as my bride, and together we are going to cleanse what remains of the Gardens of Eternity. We will start anew, like when a hunter of doves burns his fields before the hunt so that once the killing is complete, it will grow once again, both green and good. But before I do, I'm going to make one last virgin sacrifice, unto

Oblivion, and you get the privilege of being that which I offer up to him."

Xavier looked deep into the eyes of Princess Destiny. He kissed her on her forehead, her eyes closed, and she slipped into a trance. Her body went limp. She levitated up off the ground. Xavier motioned toward the empty altar prepared by the Disciples of Oblivion. The body of Princess Destiny floated toward it like a ghost.

24

THINK TANK 4-2-0

A dry river of blood ran across the back of the neck of Alexis. It was as dark as a merlot and stopped at her butterfly tattoo. On each side of Alexis sat a Scanner. Mistress LaReaux watched them all with a serpentine look in her eyes. The Drone Commander piloting the Phantom Lord opened up a communications link with the Hive.

"Hive One, this is Drone Commander do you copy?"

Inside the ziggurat, Security Drones scanned the Phantom Lord and her crew.

"Drone Commander, this is Hive," said a Communications Drone. *"Initiate Echelon."*

"Copy, Hive, initiating Echelon," replied the Drone Commander.

The Phantom Lord entered into the airspace of the ziggurat without fear of attack. The Hive's security systems stood down. The Phantom Lord landed. A Scanner unshackled Alexis from the floor and Mistress LaReaux pushed her out of the Phantom Lord. The Scanners inside the Phantom Lord exited out onto the landing pad behind them. Medical Drones unloaded Torment. Dr. Necropolis ordered the HazMat Drones in the Imperial Waste Management Transports to begin unloading the stockpile of Nekrotek. They did as he instructed while Johnny Lyes, LIVE on WXTZ Channel 13, reported that it was the Orphans of Doom that were responsible for the explosion at the Death Factory.

Elsewhere, Lieutenant Blood climbed the staircase that lead to the Temple of Oblivion. Three centurions in the Order of the Trapezoid accompanied him. With each step they took, the lustful howls of the temple prostitutes grew louder and louder. At the top, the Disciples of Oblivion, under the instruction of Mystre, prepared the naked body of Princess Destiny for the Ceremony of the Opposites. Lieutenant Blood walked passed them and into the temple.

Xavier didn't like being interrupted.

"There's a problem with General Grindcore," said Lieutenant Blood.

"What kind?" said Xavier.

"The kind you might want to have Dr. Necropolis look at," said Lieutenant Blood.

Xavier gazed into the Jewel of Wisdom and said, "Why was I not notified about the arrest of Professor Proxy?"

"Scarzensky said he'd tell you," said Lieutenant Blood.

There was an eerie silence in the temple for a moment.

"Scarzensky's dead," said Xavier. He exited the temple with Lieutenant Blood and started down the steps that lead to the Torture Garden. A dozen centurions followed in behind them.

Outside the ziggurat, atop the X-orcist, 808 exited the Super Highway and proceeded down a well-worn feeder road. He passed an old sign that read, NO UNAUTHORIZED ACCESS. The road led to a hilltop that overlooked the ancient ruins of the old city that surrounded the ziggurat on all sides. There were decaying cemeteries and graveyards everywhere.

Sassy sat perched on a broken telephone pole. She spotted 808 and landed on his shoulder. Junebug, Minx, and Officer Whistle Britches pulled up behind them in the HighRoller. They exited the vehicle. Junebug pulled out a pair of Night Crawler binoculars and zoomed in on the ziggurat.

"There she is," he said. Junebug passed the Night Crawler binoculars to Minx. She looked into the binoculars and saw Alexis step inside an elevator. The door closed in front of her. The signal transmitted to 808's Grimoire from the tracking device inside the necklace of Alexis died.

"We've got to rescue her," said Minx.

Junebug thought for a second.

"How are we gonna get inside?" he said.

Minx passed Officer Whistle Britches the Night Crawler binoculars. He adjusted the lenses. Dr. Necropolis appeared. HazMat Drones were hard at work unloading the stockpile of Nekrotek from the Imperial Waste Management Transports.

"You ever work a security detail at the ziggurat?" said Minx.

"I have," said Officer Whistle Britches. "The only way you're getting inside is in a Think Tank or some other type of authorized vehicle."

From their vantage point, Minx watched the convoys of Imperial Think Tanks from all over the city converge on the ziggurat. They merged into a single file formation when they approached the watchtowers and observation decks scattered throughout the ruins.

"I've got an idea," said Minx as a Scavenger UAV passed overhead. It scanned the area for intruders. The scan found the HighRoller. The Scavenger UAV notified the nearest Imperial Think Tank patrolling the area.

Imperial Think Tank 420 rolled down the feeder road where the HighRoller was parked. Junebug, 808, and Officer Whistle Britches hid in a graveyard next to the side of the road. They covered themselves in molecular body wraps that made their body heat undetectable. The Scavenger UAV in the sky above was unable to tell the difference between our heroes and the many dead bodies that were buried therein. When Imperial Think Tank 420 spotted the HighRoller, and the scan of the graveyard was complete, the Scavenger UAV flew off to scan the next sector scheduled for aerial surveillance.

"Hive, this is Imperial Think Tank 4-2-0. We have a civilian vehicle blocking the feeder road to the southern entrance. Do you copy?" said Specialist Percy Fryes, also known as Specialist Freedom Fries by his platoon because he wasn't known for making the greatest decisions. He was responsible for the patrols along Vector Sector D-9, where the HighRoller now sat blocking the road.

"*Think Tank 4-2-0; this is Hive. Your orders are to arrest and detain.*"

"Copy, Hive," said Specialist Fryes.

The Imperial Think Tank came to a halt.

Minx had her butt stuck out from underneath the hood of the

HighRoller and was shaking it while pretending to fix the engine. She looked up from underneath the hood. One of the security cameras affixed to the Imperial Think Tank locked-on to Minx's face and ran her likeness through the Hive's facial recognition database. It didn't take long for it to figure out who she was.

Name: Latisha Jackson
Alias: Minx
Criminal Number: 10026
Warrant Issued: Smuggling
Arrest Record: See Addendum 115269
Convictions: Possession of Star Dust with the Intent to Distribute
Note: As a minor was a ward of the Covens of the Grid, 13th District
Bounty: 1,000,000 S.C.R.I.L.L.A.
Last Known Address: 1515 McNutt Street
Relatives: Unknown

The eyes of Specialist Fryes lit up with excitement. He'd hit a lick, seven figures. A million credits all paid in scrilla was on the road right in front of him. It was all his for the taking. Specialist Fryes wasn't calling for backup on this one. There was no way he was going to share that reward with anyone. Sassy hovered above the Imperial Think Tank. With her radar, she sent out a small EMP signal that disabled the cameras and the Pitch Shifters on the Imperial Think Tank. Specialist Fryes saw the tank's systems malfunction. His camera feed of Minx disappeared. He couldn't arm the tank's Pitch Shifters. Greed had him, impatient. He'd sort the systems malfunction out after he had Minx handcuffed. Specialist Fryes jumped up from his seat and ran to the exit at the back of the tank. He was fool enough to believe that what lay before him was going to be easy pickings. The back end of the Imperial Think Tank opened up, and Specialist Fryes stepped out onto the road accompanied by two Artillery Drones. 808 silently tiptoed around the opposite side of the Think Tank without being seen and stole a Circuit Breaker out of the Think Tank's armory. About ten yards from Specialist Fryes, Minx was still shaking her bon-bon. Specialist Fryes liked what he saw. Between his raging lust and his need for greed, it's hard to say which blinded him more. Either way, he never saw what was coming next. Neither did the Artillery Drones.

"Ma'am," said Specialist Fryes. Minx didn't respond. "Ma'am, I'm going to have to ask you to step away from the vehicle. You are in an unauthorized area. I'm placing you under arrest."

Minx grinned.

"I just broke down," she said innocently. "All I need is a little help."

Specialist Fryes lunged forward to arrest Minx. 808 clobbered the two Artillery Drones with the Circuit Breaker he stole like he was holding a baseball bat. The Artillery Drones shorted out and fell to the ground. Junebug emerged from the graveyard on the opposite side of the HighRoller and pointed an AK1200 at Specialist Fryes just as he was about to cuff Minx.

"Get on the ground!" said Junebug.

Specialist Fryes motioned like he was about to reach for his gun.

Officer Whistle Britches fired up the DDT.

"I wouldn't do that if I were you," he said.

"You'll all get life in a containment cube for this!" shouted Specialist Fryes. Our heroes knew he was right, but it didn't matter, they had a friend that needed rescuing. 808 walked up behind Specialist Fryes and slapped him with the Circuit Breaker in his hand. The electrical current knocked Specialist Fryes out cold. He hit the ground like a sack of old dirty laundry and began writhing around in the dirt like an earthworm. 808 started stripping the uniform off of Specialist Fryes.

Inside Imperial Think Tank 420, the communications console was going nuts.

"Think Tank 4-2-0; this is Hive. Why is there an interruption in your visual transmission, over?"

Junebug sat down in front of the communications console.

"Hive, this is Imperial Think Tank 4-2-0," he said into the intercom. "We seem to be having a systems malfunction. My Artillery Drones have gone offline."

There was a short silence that seemed to last forever. Junebug worried, that perhaps they'd seen through Minx's plan, or worse that the Imperial Armada was sending reinforcements to arrest them all?

"Think Tank 4-2-0; this is Hive. Do you have the fugitive in custody?"

"Copy, Hive," said Junebug. "Fugitive is in custody."

The screen in front of Junebug updated.

"Think Tank 4-2-0; this is Hive. Proceed to Convoy 13."

"Copy, Hive," said Junebug. He breathed a sigh of relief. "In route to convoy."

Junebug looked at the map on his visual display and rolled Imperial Think Tank 420 toward the nearest convoy on the map, Convoy 13. Everyone was nervous, even Sassy.

"Here we go," said Officer Whistle Britches. Little did he know that in the selfsame moment Councilman Soros walked up the staircase leading to the Temple of Oblivion and passed the temple prostitutes erotically caressing one another next to the Pillars of Eternity. Once there, he beheld Princess Destiny's beautiful body laying on the Altar of the Sleeping Virgin. The Disciples of Oblivion finished preparing her naked flesh. Mystre motioned that they leave.

"I fear that Chancellor Thorn sees through the webs I weave," said Councilman Soros.

"Worry not, faithful disciple," said Mystre. "He knows not what we scheme."

"The task you have given me weighs heavily upon me," said Councilman Soros. "

"As it should," said Mystre. "The yoke of the oath you took is not for the easily broken."

"Does my work please you, Exalted Hierophant?" said Councilman Soros.

"It does," said Mystre. "Yet, your task is not complete."

"I will deliver the fool's flesh to Oblivion," said Councilman Soros.

"When thou art poor in spirit, remember what the Lord of the Void has promised thee," said Mystre. "For in that moment when he is made whole once more our master will reward thy faithful service and restore thine ancestor's lost immortality back unto thee."

25

ARMORY

Imperial Think Tank 420 merged into Convoy 13. Junebug followed the convoy into a subterranean staging area beneath the ziggurat where the Imperial Armada and the Occult Bureau processed new prisoners. Drones were marching in formation everywhere. Junebug pulled the Imperial Think Tank into a parking spot labeled *4-2-0*, and it rolled to a stop.

"What do we do now?" said Minx.

"I don't know," said Junebug.

"Don't worry," said Officer Whistle Britches. "There's an access terminal outside."

"You think it'll know where Alexis is?" said Minx.

"If anyone processed her into the ziggurat as a prisoner it will," said Officer Whistle Britches.

The brief conversation was interrupted by the intercom in the communications console.

"Think Tank 4-2-0; this is Hive. Proceed with your prisoner to Detention Level 227. A maintenance crew has been scheduled to repair the damage to your assigned Think Tank and personnel."

Junebug leaned in toward the intercom and said, "Copy, Hive."

808 handed Junebug the uniform of Specialist Fryes and walked to the back of the Think Tank to the small, yet well-equipped armory he'd

stolen the Circuit Breaker from. Everyone followed him. There were a lot of weapons back there.

Junebug liked the Behemoth, a six-barrel hand cannon, with dual clips, loaded up with thirty-two bone shattering rounds each, and a backup one-hundred and twenty-eight round high-capacity drum. It was capable of rapid dual-burst automatic firing and came equipped with a laser sight. Junebug took the Behemoth from the wall of the Imperial Think Tank with a smile.

"Now that's what I call pretty," he said.

"Watch it," said Minx. She put on a suit of F.U.R.

F.U.R. stood for, Futuristic, Ultraviolet, Reflective Camouflage.

Officer Whistle Britches filled a duffle bag full of thermite grenades.

Minx hid a gamma knife underneath her camouflage.

808 loaded up his backpack with plenty of loot as well. He'd found two Thunderclap EMP's locked away in a storage safe.

"Nice," said Officer Whistle Britches when he saw 808 with the Thunderclaps.

Once everyone was armed, Junebug finished putting on the uniform of Specialist Fryes and shackled Minx in a set of Charm Bracelets. He didn't lock them. The bay door to the back of the Imperial Think Tank opened. Sassy flew out first and flew as high as she could toward the ceiling to monitor what was going on in the staging area. Junebug, Minx, Officer Whistle Britches, and 808 exited out of the rear of the Imperial Think Tank behind her.

Floppy spotted them.

"*Rmppff!*" he attempted to bark.

808 saw Floppy jumping around in his cage like a wild animal. He was trying to get their attention. 808 signaled to Sassy to go and help him. She flew over and shot some laser beams out of her eyes. They blew the locks off of Floppy's cage. It opened. Sassy zapped the straps holding the muzzle to Floppy's face. It fell to the floor. Floppy jumped down off the cargo unit he was on and ran over to our heroes.

Officer Whistle Britches was glad to see him.

"Floppy, what are you doing here?" he said. Officer Whistle Britches knelt down to pet Floppy. "You're supposed to be with Professor Proxy."

Floppy was glad to see Officer Whistle Britches. He licked him on the face.

"Fool, will you get up?" said Junebug. He was scared they were about to blow their cover.

Officer Whistle Britches grunted and rose to his feet. Floppy scurried around his legs in a circle.

"I think he's trying to tell us something," he said. "What is it, boy? What are you trying to tell us?"

"See what he's recorded with his packet sniffer," said Minx. She'd been chased by enough of the Occult Bureau's dogs to know they recorded everything.

808 knelt down with his Grimoire and connected his Stream Ripper to Floppy's internal memory. The screen on the Grimoire started streaming a video of Professor Proxy being led down the corridor next to them to a lower level lockup with the rest of the prisoners from an Imperial Prisoner Transportation Unit.

"Looks like they've got Professor Proxy, too," said Officer Whistle Britches. He looked down at Floppy. "Is that what you were trying to tell us, boy? Did they take Professor Proxy that way?"

"*Rarf!*" barked Floppy.

"We've got to go get him," said Officer Whistle Britches.

"How you planning on rescuing him and Alexis?" said Junebug.

808 walked over to a low-level access terminal next to the parked Imperial Think Tank and plugged his Stream Ripper into an open port on the terminal. 808 initiated a search for Professor Proxy's whereabouts. His prisoner profile and a map of the ziggurat appeared on the screen of the terminal.

"They've got him locked up on Detention Level 213," said Minx as she watched the data stream over 808's shoulder.

Junebug knew the reputation of the place she was speaking of all too well.

"That's down in the Pit," he said. "Ain't nobody comes out of there alive."

"You're a real champion of hope arnt'cha?" said Minx.

"He's right," said Officer Whistle Britches. He might not have liked Junebug's choice of words, but he knew that Junebug spoke the truth. "The odds of us getting him out of there are slim to none."

Minx wasn't hearing any of the negativity.

"We're going to get him and then we're going after Alexis," she said.

"How are we supposed to get in there without them seeing us coming?" said Junebug.

"Maybe we don't have to sneak in?" said Officer Whistle Britches.

"Whatchu gettin' at Whistle Britches?" said Junebug.

"They already think we've got one prisoner," said Officer Whistle Britches. "It's not like we'd have to sneak down there to see him."

"True," said Junebug.

"808 can use his Stream Ripper to put in a fake prisoner transfer," said Officer Whistle Britches.

Minx couldn't believe she hadn't thought of it herself.

"Can you do that 808?" she said.

808 shook his head yes and got to work.

"We'll bring Minx down to the Pit under the guise that she's our prisoner, and we're transferring Professor Proxy to the same place," said Officer Whistle Britches.

Minx liked the idea.

"Sounds like a plan to me," she said.

"Me, too," said Junebug, followed by Floppy barking in approval. *"Rarf!"*

26

OBSERVATION DECK

While Junebug, Minx, Officer Whistle Britches, 808, Sassy, and Floppy planned the prison break of Professor Proxy, several floors above them, unbeknownst to them all, something much more sinister than they could all imagine was beginning to unfold. From an observation deck window inside an infirmary, Xavier watched a swarm of HazMat Drones in Hangar 18 load the barrels of Nekrotek from the Death Factory into the Star Gazer. First Lieutenant Blood, Specialist Gutts, and Corporal Gore oversaw the operation.

Dr. Necropolis scanned the broken body of General Grindcore.

"Agguhhh!" groaned General Grindcore.

Xavier was grim-faced and not amused.

"Pathetic," he said.

"I can still be of use to you," said General Grindcore.

"I have given the order to begin the extermination of everyone in the city," said Xavier. "Make sure the Medical Drones have properly inoculated every mercenary before the final purge starts. I don't want a single one of them left alive once this is over. But before you leave here, put him to sleep, then get down there with the rest of the worms, he calls help, and make sure they don't screw anything up."

Dr. Necropolis nodded that he understood Xavier's orders.

General Grindcore panicked and pleaded for mercy.

"No, please! I was loyal!" he shouted.

Xavier couldn't care less. He turned and exited the infirmary to the sounds of General Grindcore's death rattle. The sliding door of the infirmary slammed shut behind him like a coffin.

Beneath Xavier, many levels down, a personnel elevator filled with the last hope of those that inhabit what remains of the Gardens of Eternity was in the middle of finishing its descent deep down into the bowels of the ziggurat. It slid to an almost complete stop and then came to rest inside the Pit. The personnel elevator door opened. Minx stepped out. Junebug stepped out behind her. He pushed Minx along like she was a disobedient prisoner that didn't want to co-operate. Officer Whistle Britches followed behind them with 808 and Floppy by his side. Sassy popped her head out of 808's backpack. She was hidden and didn't want to blow their cover. Down the corridor, there were several Operations Drones seated at a workstation. They were responsible for monitoring every single move anything made in their hi-tech dungeon. On one of the computer monitors, Junebug and Officer Whistle Britches could be seen leading Minx toward the Operations Drones with 808 and Floppy by their side. They approached the workstation.

"We've got a prisoner transfer from Imperial Think Tank 4-2-0," said Junebug to the Operations Drone at the workstation in front of him.

"*What prisoner do you seek?*" said the Operations Drone.

"Inmate 00175858, last name Proxy," said Junebug.

Everyone was sweating bullets.

Junebug took a deep breath. Officer Whistle Britches looked down at 808 and winked.

"*4-2-0, we're going to need to verify the transfer,*" said the Operations Drone.

808 pulled out the MK Ultra Mark I & II and emptied both clips into the Operations Drones seated around the workstation.

"Good job," said Junebug.

"Now to find Professor Proxy," said Officer Whistle Britches. He sat down at the workstation. They didn't have much time. With the Operations Drones offline, it would only be a matter of time before the Hive sent reinforcements.

"You know how to work this thing?" said Junebug.

"Used to sit behind one all the time," said Officer Whistle Britches. He sealed the security barrier that led into the Pit.

Above them, in the courtyard of the Torture Garden, where if one walked the desolate path through it they would arrive at the base of the staircase that led up to the Temple of Oblivion, Mistress LaReaux waited with Alexis for Xavier to arrive. He appeared through a shielded hangar door. When Xavier saw Alexis was shackled, he motioned to Mistress LaReaux to free her.

"I did not mean for any harm to come to your robot," said Xavier. His cold-heartedness angered Alexis to no end.

"He was your son, Xavier!" she shouted back. "That evil piece of shit killed your son!"

The blazing fury in the eyes of Xavier was unreasoning. In them, you could see a demonic pain begin bubbling up to the surface like a black cauldron filled with all of the hurt he'd ever known. The words that had just come from the mouth of Alexis made him want to kill her.

"That abomination was not my son!" screamed Xavier.

27

CONTAINMENT CUBE 32

One by one, Junebug passed containment cube after containment cube, looking for Professor Proxy.

"It's cube number thirty-two!" shouted Officer Whistle Britches.

Junebug stumbled down the corridor a little faster when he heard the news. It didn't take him long to find the containment cube numbered, 32. Inside, sat Professor Proxy on the edge of his bed. His head was in his hands, and he was staring at the floor. Officer Whistle Britches could see him on one of the monitors on the workstation. He smiled and powered down the security shield of the containment cube. It flickered then disappeared.

"Professor," said Junebug as he entered the containment cube.

Professor Proxy looked up. He was shocked, almost startled.

"Junebug?" said Professor Proxy.

"Come on man, we gotta go!" said Junebug.

Professor Proxy stood up.

"How'd you get in here?" he said.

"We stole a Think Tank," said Junebug.

The two of them exited the containment cube together and made their way back down the corridor. Professor Proxy was glad to be free. When they arrived at the workstation, everyone was glad to see that he was safe. There were smiles on all of their faces.

"It's good to see all of you," said Professor Proxy.

808, Minx, Junebug, Officer Whistle Britches, Sassy, and Floppy gathered around Professor Proxy to celebrate their small yet glorious victory.

"It's good to see you, too," said Minx. She hugged Professor Proxy.

"Where is Alexis?" said Professor Proxy.

"She was taken prisoner at the Death Factory," said Officer Whistle Britches. "We followed the transport she was in, here, and the next thing we know Minx is plotting to steal a Think Tank so that we can rescue her."

"The last we saw of her she was getting into one of the ziggurat's elevators," said Minx.

"Where was the elevator going?" said Professor Proxy.

"We don't know," said Officer Whistle Britches. "That's what we were about to try and find out when we found Floppy."

"And, he lead us to you," said Minx.

"Did you find anything at the Death Factory?" said Professor Proxy.

808 took his Grimoire out of his backpack. He scrolled through the data collection app. 808 found what he was looking for. He handed the Grimoire to Professor Proxy. On the screen of the Grimoire were the videos ripped from the mainframe in the Death Factory. Professor Proxy went through the videos one by one and took a moment to absorb it all in.

"What is it?" said Officer Whistle Britches.

"This confirms my worst fear," said Professor Proxy. "While you were gone, I discovered that the Nekron you left with me was acting as a type of preservative for the nanobots, which in reality were not nanobots at all."

"What were they?" said Officer Whistle Britches.

"Nekrobiotic hatchlings," said Professor Proxy.

"What's a hatchling?" said Junebug.

"It's a type of synthetic egg from which a Nekrobyte hatches," said Professor Proxy. "In the early phases of infestation, when a host organism has no idea that they're infected, the nekrobiotic hatchlings are disguised as pharmaceutical grade nanobots that swarm inside the host's spleen. When they're finished tagging the host's DNA with a neurotransmitter, the hatchlings release Nekrotek into the host's circulatory system. This polluted blood gives the Nekrobytes a new home in which to hatch and thrive as it devours the host from the inside out and then flies off in search of other carcasses on which to feed."

"So what you're saying is that Nekron isn't a cure at all?" said Minx.

"No, it's not," said Professor Proxy. "It's spreading nekrosis, and according to the files on 808's Grimoire, it seems that Controlled Substances Incorporated has been perfecting a new experimental fast-acting form of nekrosis that is capable of changing us into a mindless, slave race of mutants, neither human nor beast."

"Why on earth would they do something like that?" said Officer Whistle Britches.

"It makes us easier to eat when we're all too dumb to run away," said Junebug.

"That's horrible," said Minx.

"When I was looking through Junebug's Night Crawler's," said Officer Whistle Britches, "I saw a swarm of HazMat Drones unloading barrels of Nekrotek from some Imperial Waste Management Transports."

"Are you sure?" said Professor Proxy.

"Sure, I'm sure," said Officer Whistle Britches. "I saw Dr. Necropolis there with it and everything."

"Did you see where they were taking it?" said Professor Proxy.

"Where it went from there, I have no way of knowing," said Officer Whistle Britches. "But I'll see what I can find."

The fingers of Officer Whistle Britches raced across the keyboard in front of him looking for any information on the location of Alexis and the missing Nekrotek. Meanwhile, in the courtyard of the Torture Garden, Xavier was still seething with disgust at the audacity of Alexis to dare to say that 808 was his child. A haunted look crawled across his face and nestled in the dark circles around his eyes. Mistress LaReaux dropped the severed head of Manzini at the feet of Xavier. Alexis looked on in horror as Manzini's dead eyes stared back at her.

"Xavier," she said. "Why?"

"Manzini participated in the killing our son," said Xavier. "I wanted you to see with your own eyes that he paid for that error in judgment with his life."

"Two wrongs don't make a right, and you know that," said Alexis. "You were raised better than to act like some butcher."

Xavier didn't care what Alexis thought about his methods. He wanted revenge and got it. An Enforcer Drone approached one of the centurions in the Order of the Trapezoid. He had a message for Xavier. The centurion closest to the Enforcer Drone took a tablet from the Enforcer Drone's hands and approached Xavier. He bowed his head like a whipped servant and presented the tablet to him. Xavier took the tablet from the centurion. A security feed of Officer Whistle Britches at the Pit's workstation surrounded by Professor Proxy, Junebug, Minx, 808, Sassy, and Floppy streamed on its screen.

"It seems that your friends are here and your little robot is still alive," said Xavier. He looked up at Mistress LaReaux. "See to them and make sure that they are brought only to me."

Mistress LaReaux bowed her head. She turned and walked away from Xavier and Alexis. A dozen centurions followed behind her. Alexis was relieved that her friends had survived the explosion at the Death Factory and that 808 was still alive. In her heart, a new thought did stir filled with worry. She reached up and reset the tracking device on her necklace. Alexis prayed it would be able to sync with 808, and that her friends would come to her rescue. Without them, she feared she would not be able to escape on her own.

28

VAULT BREAKER

Down in the Pit, there was a loud clanging sound that made everyone jump. Officer Whistle Britches could see Mistress LaReaux, a swarm of drones, and at least a dozen centurions standing on the other side of the Pit's security barrier via one of the security feeds on the monitor on the workstation in front of him. A pair of Demolition Drones had placed a Vault Breaker against the security barrier. It was only a matter of time before they got through.

"It's the welcome wagon," said Officer Whistle Britches.

The center of the security barrier slowly turned red.

"We've gotta get out of here," said Junebug.

"The only way back to the elevator is through that security barrier," said Minx.

Officer Whistle Britches stood up from the workstation and powered up the DDT.

"Stand back," he said.

Officer Whistle Britches walked out in front of the workstation and blew a hole in the floor of the Pit with the DDT.

"I see you've begun to get the hang of it," said Professor Proxy.

Officer Whistle Britches smiled and powered down the DDT.

808 tugged at Professor Proxy's lab coat. Professor Proxy looked down at 808. 808 pointed to a flashing heart-shaped icon on the

screen of his Grimoire. It was the tracking device in the necklace of Alexis.

"808 just received confirmation of the location of Alexis," said Professor Proxy. "She's in the Torture Garden."

"That's at the very top of the ziggurat," said Officer Whistle Britches.

"Our cover's blown," said Junebug, "to get there we'd have to take on the whole Hive."

"We won't have to if we shut down the Hive's power source," said Officer Whistle Britches. He sat back down and pulled up a security schematic of the ziggurat on the workstation in front of him. "If we disable the tryptamine reactor at the center of the ziggurat, we stand a fighting chance."

"How are we gonna do that?" said Minx.

808 placed his backpack next to the workstation and unzipped it. Inside the backpack were the two Thunderclap EMPs from the armory of Imperial Think Tank 420.

"It seems 808 has come prepared for such an occasion," said Professor Proxy.

Everyone gathered around the workstation was pleased with 808 for being so forward thinking.

"There are four security nodes located in four separate protocol suites that power the security shield protecting the tryptamine reactor," said Officer Whistle Britches. "The tryptamine reactor powering the Hive is thirteen levels above the security nodes inside the Occult Bureau's central command center. It's also the location of the Hive's central mainframe supercomputer. If you want to get past the security shield and get inside the central command center, you're going to have to disable all of the security nodes. It's the only way to get close enough to the mainframe to plant the Thunderclaps and blow the reactor. Once you blow the reactor, anything connected to the Hive's central mainframe supercomputer will go offline and shutdown."

"It'll be harder to catch all of us if we split up," said Minx.

"It'll be even harder to catch us if we let the prisoners in these cubes loose," said Officer Whistle Britches.

Everybody liked the idea even if it was dangerous.

"Here's what we're going to do," said Professor Proxy. "Junebug, you and Minx, disable the security nodes in the southern and western zones, Whistle Britches you'll be responsible for the security node in the northern zone, while 808 and myself will be responsible for disabling the security node in the eastern zone."

"Floppy you go with'em," said Officer Whistle Britches.

"*Rarf!*" barked Floppy.

"When they've all been disabled," said Professor Proxy, "we will rendezvous at the reactor, plant the Thunderclaps, and then make our way up to the top of the ziggurat where we will attempt to free Alexis."

Officer Whistle Britches opened his duffle bag filled with thermite grenades from the armory of Imperial Think Tank 420.

"Take a few of these with you," he said. "I'll stay here for as long as I can and reinforce the security barrier with the DDT."

"Sounds like a plan," said Junebug.

808 nodded in agreement and placed several thermite grenades inside his backpack while the map of the ziggurat on his Grimoire updated. Officer Whistle Britches, Junebug, and Minx synced their communicators and put them in their pockets. Sassy updated her radar. Floppy updated his packet sniffer.

808 strapped his backpack on and jumped down the hole in the floor of the Pit. Floppy jumped in the hole after 808, then Professor Proxy. Once they were on the level below the Pit, they ran down the corridor that led to the personnel elevator that would take them to the eastern zone.

Officer Whistle Britches took a couple of thermite grenades out of the duffle bag and put them in his pockets as he looked at Junebug and Minx.

"There's a personnel elevator one sector over, that leads down into an armory, that is right next to the protocol suite of the southern zone," he said. "From there it's a hop, skip, and a jump to the western zone. The two of you get moving. I'll meet up with you at the reactor."

"Don't lollygag," said Junebug.

"Yeah," said Minx. "Once we're out of sight you hurry up and get going."

"I will," said Officer Whistle Britches. "Now go on, get!"

Junebug grabbed the duffle bag full of thermite grenades and jumped down the hole created by Officer Whistle Britches with the DDT. Minx jumped in behind him. Once they were on the level below the Pit, they ran down the corridor that led to the personnel elevator that would take them to the southern zone. Sassy flew through the air in front of them and led the way.

Officer Whistle Britches knew that it was only a matter of time before Mistress LaReaux cut through the security barrier with the Vault Breaker. Once Junebug and Minx were gone, Officer Whistle Britches walked over to the sealed security barrier of the Pit. He armed the DDT. On the wall next to the security barrier was a control panel. Officer Whistle Britches pressed the button labeled, REINFORCEMENT. Upon its pressing, two additional shield doors slammed shut.

Mistress LaReaux heard the additional reinforcement of the shield doors as they echoed closed. It made her even more determined to get inside. The Demolition Drones increased the power of the Vault Breaker to its maximum capacity.

Officer Whistle Britches adjusted the DDT and lowered the energy settings to something that was a little less destructive than its default capabilities. Slowly, he fanned the DDT with a steady blast of quantum energy across the reinforced shield doors, melting them into one fused mass. Officer Whistle Britches walked back over to the Pit's workstation, opened all of the containment cubes, and jumped into the hole he'd created with the DDT. Once he was on the level below the Pit, he ran off down the corridor toward the personnel elevator that would take him to the security node in the northern zone.

Several minutes later, the Vault Breaker ripped a hole through the metallic mess Officer Whistle Britches made of the reinforced shield doors. A swarm of Security Drones stepped through first. Mistress LaReaux entered the Pit behind them followed by a dozen centurions. She knew that she'd been had before the smoke cleared. Inmates were running everywhere and looking for a way to escape the Pit. Some were pouring down the hole in the floor. The swarm of Security Drones opened fire with their Baphomets. Mistress LaReaux and the centurions that were with her battled their way to the Pit's workstation. Once there, displayed on the monitors on the workstation, Mistress LaReaux could see Officer Whistle Britches, 808, Floppy, and Professor Proxy scattering down their respective corridors. Junebug, Minx, and Sassy were in an elevator descending into the southern zone. Mistress LaReaux stormed away from the workstation and continued her pursuit.

29

TORTURE GARDEN

The hour was late. Together, Xavier and Alexis walked through the Torture Garden guarded by a dozen centurions in the Order of the Trapezoid. A spirit of unease hung in the thick humid air all around them.

"Where are we going?" said Alexis.

"You'll see," said Xavier.

They came to the center of the Torture Garden where there was a strange-looking mausoleum. Statues of weird creatures and ominous things adorned its exterior. A centurion walked up the steps of the mausoleum and opened the door to the crypt. Xavier walked inside. Alexis was hesitant. Xavier gave her an assuring look. Alexis walked inside. In the crypt, it was dark, as dark as the sky at night without a single star in the heavens. Alexis saw a soft, faint light in the distance. As she made her way through the darkness, Alexis could see that the petals of a strange, yet beautiful flower, surrounding a sarcophagus, was the source of the light.

Inscribed on the sarcophagus were the words,

MASTER OV THE ANCIENT ELECTRONIC ARTS

"Is that the sarcophagus of Oblivion?" said Alexis.

"Indeed, it is," said Xavier. He reached down and plucked one of the flowers surrounding the sarcophagus. "But the real question is do you know what this is?"

"I've never seen a flower like that before," said Alexis.

"It's a skull flower," said Xavier.

"Really?" said Alexis.

"Do you know what makes them so special?" said Xavier.

"Their glowing petals?" said Alexis.

"Yes," said Xavier as he held back laughter, "their petals make them special. But the flower also contains the cure for nekrosis."

"How?" said Alexis.

"Their blossom contains a resin. It pours out like blood and kills the plant when harvested," said Xavier. "The blood of a skull flower purifies the body, every single cell. Mystre gave me a vial full of it when you were in the hospital. I used it to save your life."

Alexis was shocked.

"Mystre saved my life?" she said.

"Without his assistance," said Xavier, "you would have died."

Alexis was silent for a moment and then said, "When I was in the Death Factory I saw a video of a pregnant woman that worked in the tryptamine mines in the Golden Triangle. A swarm of hatchlings swarmed inside her spleen. When they hatched into Nekrobytes, her spleen burst open, and Nekrotek polluted her circulatory system. The swarm devoured her body from the inside out as a single Nekrobyte attached itself to the child's brainstem. It tore its mother's stomach open and crawled out from inside her like some evil spawn hidden away in the darkest corners of the Void. The child didn't even look human. It was a mutated monster. As I watched the video, I thought to myself, why was I spared her fate?"

"Hatchlings are capable of gene editing," said Xavier. "They were given this capability so that those infected could be cataloged and tracked. Your mother's people never mingled their bloodline with the Immortals that sat upon the Divine Council of the Great Architect of the Universe. Your father was a direct descendant of Oblivion and Psydonia. Your blood type is rather unique for as you well know your father and I are the only ones of our bloodline to have ever mingled their seed with the genetics of an inhabitant of the Golden Triangle and their offspring. The hatchlings didn't know what to do with you or our son, so they didn't tag either of you, but they did malfunction and alter his physiology."

"So you admit that he is your son?" said Alexis.

"I admit that is my fault that you had a miscarriage," said Xavier. "When the hatchlings inside your spleen released the Nekrotek inside them, they poisoned your body. I should have never let you near that Nekron. Without Mystre's help, a slow-growing and debilitating form of nekrosis similar to the type developed by those that work in the tryptamine mines was to be your fate. You were fortunate that many of the Nekrobytes never hatched. It kept the Nekrotek in your circulatory system to a minimum. The ones that didn't attack you or our son were still in hibernation mode and just floated through your body along with the hatchlings. They did not attack you because they are programmed only to kill those who are not of the bloodline of Oblivion and Psydonia."

"Why are you involved in the creation of such an evil thing?" said Alexis.

"Before my father died," said Xavier, "he arranged for me to meet with Councilman Soros about our family investing in Controlled Substances Incorporated and finding a solution to its problems with the Emissions Guild. The refinement of tryptamine crystals for use as a source of energy is a filthy and toxic process. To call Zohar polluted is an understatement. The Emissions Guild had been studying the effects of the pollution on those living in Zohar for quite some time. Their study concluded that the rate of patients with nekrotik tumors was skyrocketing. The main cause they said was Industrial Plant No. 213. The Occult Bureau opened an investigation into what Manzini knew about the problem and placed Special Agent Scarzensky in charge of the case. Manzini found himself under the threat of indictment and Controlled Substances Incorporated was facing heavy fines, possibly even bankruptcy."

"So he wanted you to bail Manzini out?" said Alexis.

"Yes," said Xavier, "he'd spoken with General Grindcore and Manzini about the possibility of arming some of the Armada's elite death squad mercenaries with some of Controlled Substances Incorporated's experimental chemical and biological weapons. Their mission would be to disguise themselves as terrorists and launch attacks not only on the tryptamine mines in the Golden Triangle but on the local population as well. The inevitable refugee crisis would give General Grindcore an excuse to invade the Golden Triangle and seize the tryptamine deposits therein. If Manzini were bankrupt or in a containment cube, it would be impossible to arm his death squad. To ensure that the invasion was a success we discussed the need for me to fund the operation off the books and fill my father's soon to be vacant office, Manzini was willing to sell me a seat on the board of directors and forty-nine percent of his share in Controlled Substances Incorporated for my help. To garner political support for the venture, Councilman Soros promised that he would rally support for me on the Supreme Council and see to it that a blind eye was turned to the machinations of a select few in the House of the Black Widow, so that I could spread my families fortune amongst those who not only needed financial support in their re-election campaigns but were of one mind and predisposed to operate in one accord with our vision of the future."

"You bribed them?" said Alexis.

"Bribed is such a vulgar word," said Xavier. "It insinuates that somehow I did something corrupt. I assure you, every single member of the House of the Black Widow I gave money to was already standing there with their hand out. You cannot corrupt that which has already been corrupted. All one can do is realize that it's in their best interest to give that hand what it wants before someone else does."

"What you did was illegal," said Alexis.

"Or customary," said Xavier, "depending on how bad it is that you want what you want."

"What about the Emissions Guild?" said Alexis. "Did you bribe them, too?"

"Before I promised Manzini anything," said Xavier, "I wanted to see what weapons Controlled Substances Incorporated had at its disposal. Once I was sure that the operation could be pulled off I met with the Emissions Guild and they all agreed that it was in their best interest to recommend that the Occult Bureau kill their inquiry into Manzini and Industrial Plant No. 213."

"How much did that cost you?" said Alexis.

"Nothing in the whole scheme of things," said Xavier.

"Don't play coy with me," said Alexis.

"I gave each of them whatever they wanted, and you'd be shocked at how little some asked for," said Xavier. "I also promised them that when I became chancellor and the Golden Triangle was annexed as a province that each elected official on the Emissions Guild would receive a small percentage of the gross earnings from its exploitation. To reassure their fears that they would not be locked away in a containment cube for being involved in such a venture I let them know that my first order of business would be to ensure that not a single grain of sand in the Golden Triangle would ever be considered part of the empire. Its legal status in the eyes of the House of the Black Widow would forever remain that of a conquered territory without a single legal right under imperial law. The land, people, and resources would be ours to do with as we pleased."

"Slavery?" said Alexis.

"Slavery was never discussed," said Xavier. "However, Councilman Soros did make it very clear that he wanted the inhabitants of the Golden Triangle eliminated from the equation. Once the Orphans of Doom saw to it that everyone was infected, and General Grindcore cleansed the land, the plan was to send in Mining Drones to do all the work."

"Why kill my mother's people?" said Alexis.

"To some," said Xavier, "their death is of a ritual significance that the profane have a hard time comprehending. The easier pill to swallow is if they're all dead there is no one left for the soft-hearted to scream to the House of the Black Widow about how we needed to end our inhumane incursion into the Golden Triangle and cease our mining operations."

"You should all be locked away in containment cubes for the rest of your lives for what you've done," said Alexis.

"Without those deposits," said Xavier, "the empire would cease to function."

"Zohar has more than enough tryptamine to power the empire," said Alexis. "There's no excuse for what you did."

"My families mining operations ripped the last Zoharian crystal from the ground beneath what remains of the Gardens of Eternity six month's after the invasion," said Xavier. "The Supreme Council has been powering the empire with imported tryptamine ever since."

"Everyone involved in this conspiracy," said Alexis, "would have been a lot better off just coming clean and telling the citizenry about the energy crisis the empire was facing so that a peaceful trade agreement could have been arranged instead of a war."

"Perhaps," said Xavier, "but at the time it seemed like the right course of action."

"What did your father say when you told him what Councilman Soros had proposed?" said Alexis.

"He was pleased that Manzini was willing to sell us a piece of his operation," said Xavier. "Our family on many an occasion had attempted to do business with the Manzini family, but they were reluctant."

Alexis saw something move in the shadows out of the corner of her eye.

"Did you see that?" she said.

"See what?" said Xavier.

"Something just moved in the shadows?" said Alexis.

"It was probably a rat," said Xavier.

"No, this was something much larger," said Alexis.

"What did it look like?" said Xavier.

"A spider," said Alexis.

Xavier watched Alexis peer into the darkness, hoping to catch a glimpse of whatever it was she thought she'd seen.

"Do you want me to continue," he said, "or do you wish that I would go forth into the darkness and see what ghoul hides in the shadows of where the bones of our ancestor grow old?"

"You were telling me about Manzini," said Alexis while she continued to stare out into the shadows of the crypt.

"Controlled Substances Incorporated was deeply in debt to the Imperial Central Bank," said Xavier. "The rumors amongst the board of governors was that Manzini's drug and sex addictions were crippling his company financially, and there was some truth in what they were saying, but it wasn't the whole story. His dirty little secret was that his desire to find a cure for his nekrosis is what brought his company to its knees."

"Manzini had nekrosis?" said Alexis.

"The liver spots he claimed that were on his hands due to old age were the scars of the chancres he'd lanced in a futile effort to conceal the disease," said Xavier.

"Destiny spoke of them earlier tonight when I was with her at the Crystal Ball," said Alexis.

"The worthless piece of shit told that lie to every fool dumb enough to believe it that he came in contact with," said Xavier. "Nekron was in all actuality Manzini's futile attempt at trying to find a cure for himself. He'd pumped billions into the Research and Development Division of Controlled Substances Incorporated in the futile hope that it would bear fruit. As a cure or treatment, Nekron's useless, but as a preservative for nekrobiotic hatchlings, it's perfect. It wasn't until you got sick that Mystre presented us with a viable cure for nekrosis that we called, Halcyon 1138."

"I saw some vials of it in the lab of Dr. Necropolis," said Alexis.

"It's just a fancy way of saying the blood of skull flowers mixed with the proper amount of their petal dew, but Halcyon 1138 sounds much more professional don't you think?" said Xavier.

"I figured it was something he used in the creation of the grotesque things he had stuffed in all those cryotubes," said Alexis.

"The play pretties of Dr. Necropolis are an entirely different beast unto themselves," said Xavier. "His mind and his motives are not easily understood unlike Manzini's who irregardless of the fact that he was a dying man made it very clear that in exchange for his involvement in Councilman Soros' plan that he didn't want to have to ever bid on an imperial contract before the House of the Black Widow ever again and he wanted the Emissions Guild off his back, forever."

"I can only imagine what you did to keep my father from discovering that," said Alexis.

"What I proposed to Manzini was that we create a bunch of dummy corporations so that it didn't look like I rigged the bidding on any imperial contracts in favor of a company I had a vested interest in," said Xavier. "No one ever needed to know that after the invasion that it was Controlled Substances Incorporated operating in the Golden Triangle. Once I became chancellor, I could ensure that the House of the Black Widow would be responsible for all of the costs associated with the venture and that all the monies they received from the Imperial Central Bank to fund the operations in the Golden Triangle would be funneled first through the dummy corporations and then into the coffers of Controlled Substances Incorporated for providing support contracts in the region. Once the tryptamine flowed back across the border, I repackaged and sold our ill-gotten gains as Zoharian tryptamine."

"What made you think that was a good idea?" said Alexis.

"My family has been hiding their dealings in the Golden Triangle for as long as people have known that there was tryptamine beneath it," said Xavier. "You knew this when you chose to become my wife. What you chose to hide from your father was not of my doing."

"I didn't know that you were going to commit genocide," said Alexis.

"I told you, the tryptamine within the empire's borders was running out," said Xavier. "Something had to be done. The fortune and future of our family was at stake."

"And so you chose a path that would destroy it?" said Alexis.

"At the time my thinking was that the vast majority of the Golden Triangle was an untapped resource of immeasurable wealth," said Xavier, "and whoever controlled those tryptamine deposits would rule this empire forever."

"I don't know how you can live with yourself," said Alexis.

"Every moment of my life I wish I wouldn't have agreed to meet with Councilman Soros," said Xavier. "I hate myself for what I have done to our family, to our child, I'd be lying to you if I didn't admit that I became sick to my stomach when I saw the Nekrobytes for the first time."

"And why is that?" said Alexis.

"I expected a more traditional weapon, I suppose," said Xavier.

"Not a cybernetic organism?" said Alexis.

"It never even crossed my mind," said Xavier. "Dr. Necropolis told me he originally designed the Nekrobytes to act as an artificial maggotoid that would feed off of the toxic byproducts made during the tryptamine refinement process."

"They were decontamination bots?" said Alexis.

"Dr. Necropolis was the first to observe that maggotoids not only feast on tryptamine crystals but if placed on nekrotik flesh that the grotesque creatures would devour any trace of nekrosis in the diseased body of the afflicted," said Xavier. "It was his idea to reprogram the operating system of the Nekrobytes to feed on the nekrotik flesh of infected people. He miniaturized the Nekrobytes and hid them inside pharmaceutical grade nanobots as hatchlings to add an element of stealth to their many features. To make the Nekrobytes a more effective killing machine when they hatched he programmed them to feed on the nekrotik flesh and tumors of the host organisms body and use it as a fuel by which to grow larger and larger until it completely devoured the individual. Each of the Orphans of Doom, including Viirus, were hand-picked by General Grindcore and implanted with a Nekrobyte at the request of the Councilman Soros. But that was nothing compared to the final part of his plan."

"And what was that?" said Alexis.

"The implementation of hatchlings in the food supply," said Xavier.

"You put hatchlings in the food supply?" said Alexis.

"The Immortal Kingdoms, for the most part, have been completely infected," said Xavier. "Their entire food supply contains hatchlings. Many of the inhabitants of the Golden Triangle were infected as well if they ate imported food from those lands."

"What about Zohar?" said Alexis.

"We kept the exposure to those dwelling in Zohar to a minimum," said Xavier. "Hence the need for the forced inoculations. If an inhabitant of Zohar traveled to one of the Immortal Kingdoms and ate while they were there, then yes, they're infected. It's why this evening when the Orphans of Doom attacked the Crystal Ball I wasn't worried about you being exposed to Nekrotek. We didn't use any."

"If the canisters didn't contain Nekrotek what did they contain?" said Alexis.

"A harmless accelerant," said Xavier. "If someone had been exposed in the Immortal Kingdoms or while traveling to the Golden Triangle, the hatchlings were programmed to lay dormant in the host until given the signal to hatch by the Hive or if exposed to an accelerant, whichever came first. The accelerant at the Crystal Ball activated the hatchlings already inside of the infected giving anyone who laid eyes on the exposed this evening the impression that an actual terrorist attack took place."

"Had I known what your family was truly involved in," said Alexis, "I would have never agreed to marry you."

"It seems we both live with regret then," said Xavier. "I take no pleasure in saying this, but no matter what you may think about your father, in truth, he was not much different than mine."

"My father was nothing like yours," said Alexis.

"The House of the Black Widow heavily subsidizes your families vineyards just like our tryptamine mines," said Xavier. "I'll admit that your father was anything but poor, but were it not for my father's generosity he would have been left to rot as a lowly and little-respected representative in some lonely far corner of that elected body. Your father was made one of the governor's of the Imperial Central Bank because of my love for you."

"That's not true," said Alexis.

"Believe whatever you want," said Xavier. "When I told my father you were pregnant he offered the position to your father as an act of good faith that our family had every intention of doing right by not only you but him. As long as your father got what he wanted he never uttered a word of contempt in my families direction."

"I could have died, Xavier," said Alexis. "Did you really think that he would keep his mouth shut when he realized what you were doing?"

"He took an oath," said Xavier.

"And so you had him killed?" said Alexis.

"I did not have your father killed," said Xavier. "Nor did I want anything to do with it."

"So you knew?" said Alexis.

"I warned your father on more than one occasion long before I invested in Controlled Substances Incorporated that he should let his interest in the Occult Bureau's investigation into Manzini go," said Xavier. "It was none of his business, and my father even advised him that to meddle in such an affair could kill his political career. His environmental stances when he served in the House of the Black Widow pleased no one. What you fail to understand is that when your father accepted his post as a governor of the Imperial Central Bank, he became a new creature not only in the eyes of Oblivion but in the eyes of everyone involved with the hidden inner workings of the empire. It is one thing to be a wine merchant. It's an honest living. Favors are needed from time to time, partnerships to be trustworthy, and agreements always honored. It is an ancient and honorable profession. However, there are no oaths that need to be made to cultivate a grape. The same holds true for the House of the Black Widow, it is a place where any profane man or woman can buy a seat and rattle off a few words about how they promise to the put the people of the empire first in everything they do, yet somehow the pocket of the pauper is never lined. I know that you have never stepped foot inside the temple, nor did your father properly instruct you in the ways of those that gather therein. All one needs to know when they stand outside its entrance is to look up and see thine only commandment, don't break the oath. It didn't matter how your father felt, how angry or hurt he was, nor did it matter how wronged he may have very well been. Irregardless of the vain religious musings he thought he kept secret from those therein when he attempted to honor your dead mother by gallivanting around as a follower of the Great Architect of the Universe, my beloved, when I tell you this, I tell you only because it is the cold hard truth of the matter, when you bend that knee, it is only the will of Oblivion that matters. Nothing else."

Alexis took a deep breath and said, "Who gave the order to have my father killed?"

"Councilman Soros," said Xavier.

"Did he ever discuss it with you?" said Alexis.

"Yes," said Xavier.

"When?" said Alexis.

"Earlier this evening when I was in the valet," said Xavier.

"Was he involved in Manzini's plot to kill us at the refugee camp?" said Alexis.

"Yes," said Xavier, "Manzini claimed Councilman Soros paid him to do it."

"Did he tell you why?" said Alexis.

"No," said Xavier. "But let me make this abundantly clear when you and your father went to the refugee camp the two of you were supposed to take a placebo, nothing more. Neither one of you was ever supposed to be hurt. I had no hand in what happened nor did I have any knowledge that something like that was about to take place."

Their conversation was interrupted by the sound of the doors of the mausoleum opening. Xavier and Alexis heard several pairs of footsteps and the sound of a metal staff hitting the floor of the mausoleum as the footsteps grew closer and closer. The shadows grew silent, and Mystre stepped into the soft pale light of the skull flowers surrounding the sarcophagus of Oblivion along with several of his disciples and said, "It is time."

30

TRYPTAMINE REACTOR

In the eastern zone of the ziggurat, 808 peeked his head around the corner of the sector he was entering to see if there were any Security Drones on patrol. He could hear the hum of the security node in the distance. There was no one around. 808 ran across the walkway. Professor Proxy followed behind him with Floppy by his side. They were cautious and alert for any sign of danger. The hum was getting louder. 808 stopped for a moment and looked at the map on his Grimoire.

"We should be getting close," said Professor Proxy.

808 nodded in agreement and ran towards the hum. Professor Proxy and Floppy followed behind him. They ran for a few seconds. Floppy spotted something. Professor Proxy stopped dead in his tracks and hid. It was a swarm of Security Drones. Killer was walking with them. He stopped for a moment and looked around. Killer could sense something was up but couldn't tell what. Professor Proxy and Floppy waited until they were out of sight. Once they were gone, Professor Proxy and Floppy ran across the final walkway together and down the corridor leading into the protocol suite housing the eastern security node. 808 was inside. He handed a thermite grenade to Professor Proxy.

"Careful," said Professor Proxy.

Floppy kept watch.

Once they were planted, 808 and Professor Proxy set the timers on the thermite grenades and ran off toward the center of the ziggurat. Floppy ran alongside them. The location of a personnel elevator that could take them to the tryptamine reactor was blinking on the map on 808's Grimoire.

In an elevator descending into the southern zone, Junebug was having problems with his communicator.

"What's the matter?" said Minx.

"The signal's cutting in and out," said Junebug. Nothing he did helped the signal to clear up. The elevator came to its final destination and stopped. The elevator doors opened. Sassy fluttered out first. Junebug exited behind her, followed by Minx. To the east of them, the sound of the thermite grenades 808 and Professor Proxy placed in the protocol suite of the eastern zone could be heard rumbling in the distance as they exploded.

"Sounds like 808 and Professor Proxy were successful," said Minx.

Even though it was a small moment of victory, Junebug was hesitant to begin celebrating.

"Let's hurry up and get this over with," he said.

Minx nodded in agreement.

Once they got to the protocol suite housing the southern security node, Junebug and Minx planted the thermite grenades and set their timers. Minx was the first to get done.

"You done on your side?" she said.

Junebug finalized his timer settings, and the countdown began.

"Yeah," he said. "Let's get out of here."

When Junebug and Minx turned to exit, there standing before them, was Mistress LaReaux with a swarm drones and a dozen centurions. Junebug opened fire with the Behemoth.

Boom! Boom! Boom! Boom! Boom! Boom!

Junebug's whole body shook with every shot. With state-of-the-art precision, he blew massive holes in the armor of each and every Security Drone the targeting system of the Behemoth locked-on. Mistress LaReaux returned fire. Lasers ripped through everything around them. One hit the wall next to Minx causing a control panel to explode. Minx threw up her arms to shield her face. Junebug grabbed her and ducked for cover.

"You okay?" he said.

"Yeah," said Minx. There was a latch to a patch panel on the floor beneath her. She opened it and could see that it led into an energy re-distribution network.

"Cover me while I head to next protocol suite," she said.

Junebug sprayed several rounds from the Behemoth at the Security Drones that continued to attempt to swarm into the protocol suite. He could see that Minx had a small cut on her forehead. It was beginning to bleed a little. He licked his thumb and wiped away the blood so that it didn't begin to dribble down into her eye.

"It's bad juju for us to split up like that," said Junebug.

"You go ahead of me and meet up with Professor Proxy and 808?" said Minx.

"I'm not leaving you," said Junebug.

Minx put her head against his forehead like two puppies about to wrestle and looked deep into Junebug's eyes.

"I've got this," she said. Minx looked at Sassy. "Sassy you stay with him."

"*Squawk!*" said Sassy. She understood she was going to have to be Junebug's extra set of eyes and ears while Minx was gone.

Minx kissed Junebug on the lips, powered up her camouflage, and disappeared.

Junebug opened fire with the Behemoth.

Boom! Boom! Boom! Boom! Boom! Boom!

A half-dozen Security Drones exploded.

The timers on the thermite grenades were about to expire.

Junebug looked at Sassy and said, "Come on, let's get out of here."

Junebug jumped down the patch panel of the protocol suite and into the energy re-distribution network. The gunfire from Mistress LaReaux's Tombstone whizzed passed him. Junebug hit the floor of the energy re-distribution network hard. His ankles felt like they were about to break. Junebug got up, limped around for a moment, and started running for his life.

Mistress LaReaux gave the command to cease fire. Everyone did as commanded. A Security Drone approached Mistress LaReaux with a scan of the protocol suite displayed on its visor. No life-forms of any kind were detected. Two Security Drones entered the protocol suite. One Security Drone gave the signal that Junebug, Minx, and Sassy had escaped, the other Security Drone spotted the thermite grenades. They exploded. Mistress LaReaux flew backward. Half of the centurions that were with her died. An equal number of the drones struggled to stay online or found themselves damaged beyond repair.

The southern zone of the ziggurat filled with smoke.

Mistress LaReaux rose to her feet. A damaged Security Drone approached her. Across its cracked visor, a security feed of Minx crawling out of one of the energy re-distribution network's patch panels started streaming. Her camouflage was uncloaking. She was only a few sectors away from the entrance to the western zone and its protocol suite. Mistress LaReaux motioned to the remaining centurions that were still alive to follow her. She would have her revenge for this momentary defeat, and she planned on taking it out of Minx's hide.

In the selfsame moment, in the northern zone, Officer Whistle Britches ran as fast as he could. Through sector after sector, Officer Whistle Britches huffed and puffed. At any moment he hoped he would find the protocol suite housing the northern security node. The map on his communicator phased in and out.

"Where is it? Where is it? Where is it?" Officer Whistle Britches said to himself. He looked in every direction for the protocol suite. "Come on. I know it's here somewhere."

Officer Whistle Britches couldn't make any sense of the map. His frustration grew as it continued to phase in and out on the screen of the communicator in his hand. It warped and phased back into its proper form. The display cleared. Officer Whistle Britches could faintly hear the hum of the security node.

"Yes!" he said to himself.

Officer Whistle Britches ran inside the protocol suite. He planted the thermite grenades around the northern security node and armed their timers. The clicking sound of the boots of a swarm of Security Drones was coming his way. There was only one way in or out of the protocol suite. The Security Drones would see him if he tried to run for it. Officer Whistle Britches was trapped. As all began to look hopeless, he noticed a patch panel on the floor. Officer Whistle Britches grabbed the latch and gave it a good pull. It was stuck. Officer Whistle Britches took out a multi-purpose utility tool from his pocket and clicked open a mechanical screwdriver. The boots of the swarm of Security Drones getting closer echoed outside. It sounded like the swarm was about to be on top of him at any moment if he didn't hurry. Officer Whistle Britches removed the first screw. The loose screw stayed magnetized to the end of the screwdriver. The clicking sound of the Security Drones boots continued to get closer and closer.

"Come on, come on!" said Officer Whistle Britches underneath his breath. His forehead was beginning to pour with sweat. The timers on the thermite grenades raced down. One by one he removed the remaining screws. Officer Whistle Britches yanked the patch panel on the floor. It flew open. Officer Whistle Britches stuck the screws in his pocket and crawled inside. When they marched by the explosion of the detonating thermite grenades consumed the Security Drones. The network coils all around Officer Whistle Britches started to shut down. He breathed a sigh of relief. Officer Whistle Britches noticed a sign on the wall of the energy re-distribution network that read, VENTILATION SYSTEM. He figured it would only be a matter of time before the Hive discovered his location. If nothing else, a crew of Maintenance Drones would be dispatched to his location to repair the destroyed node and bring it back online. There'd be no one patrolling the ventilation system, though.

Once more, Officer Whistle Britches removed the multi-purpose utility tool from his pocket and proceeded to remove the damaged vent from the wall in front of him. It fell to the floor with a loud bang. Officer Whistle Britches grunted to himself and crawled inside. Our tubby hero wiggled and rolled around for what seemed like an eternity until he came to the end of the ventilation shaft. It too had a vent on it. Officer Whistle Britches removed it and lost his grip on the loose vent. It fell into the abyss below. Officer Whistle Britches poked his head out of the open vent and looked around. The artificial wind made by the ziggurat's cooling system hit him in the face and blew his officer's cap off the top of his head. Officer Whistle Britches dared not look down as he pulled himself out of the ventilation shaft. It was time to hoof it.

"Gravity Boots don't fail me now," said Officer Whistle Britches. The Gravity Boots on his feet locked-on to the metallic exterior of the

ventilation system, and he started his long walk up the interior of the
ziggurat to the tryptamine reactor above him.

Back in the western zone, Minx entered the protocol suite housing
the final security node. She placed the thermite grenades. All was
going according to plan, Minx armed the timers. In the distance, she
could hear the footsteps of someone fast approaching. Minx fired the
wrist launcher on her Claw at the ceiling and hoisted herself up and
out of sight just as Mistress LaReaux entered the protocol suite. She
knew Minx was still there, but where? Mistress LaReaux stood on the
floor beneath Minx, clueless to her whereabouts. Minx slowly lowered
herself down. As she dangled above Mistress LaReaux, a droplet of
blood from the cut on her forehead trickled down her flesh. It fell and
hit the skin of Mistress LaReaux. She looked up. Minx pounced in a
lethal display of prowess. The attack took Mistress LaReaux by
surprise. She dropped the Tombstone revolver in her hand. The two of
them rolled across the floor together until Mistress LaReaux kicked
Minx off of her. Minx tossed a thermite grenade, and it detonated right
outside the protocol suite's entrance. The explosion killed all the
remaining drones and centurions that were with Mistress LaReaux.
Mistress LaReaux pulled out her machete and swung it at Minx. The
blade of the Huntress found flesh.

"Aagghh!" Minx cried out in pain. The camouflage she had on
flickered. It was damaged and wouldn't turn back on. Minx was cut
both deep and wide on her side. She couldn't hide. Mistress LaReaux
hissed at Minx. Minx reached for the gamma knife she had hidden. She
swiped the gamma knife at Mistress LaReaux and missed. Mistress
LaReaux swung the Huntress at Minx over and over again barely
missing her every time. She swung one too many times and lost her
balance. Minx kicked Mistress LaReaux. She hit a wall on the opposite
side of the room so hard that it put a hole in it. Mistress LaReaux
dropped the Huntress. Minx threw the gamma knife in her hand. The
blade hit Mistress LaReaux in the center of her skull. Her eyes rolled
into the back of her head. She was dead, or so it seemed. Mistress
LaReaux shape-shifted and became a snake. Minx couldn't believe her
eyes. The snake slithered off into a vent cooling the protocol suite.

Minx was bleeding pretty bad. The wound on her side was already
beginning to fester and look infected. The pain was agonizing.

Mistress LaReaux had laced the blade of the Huntress with poison, what it was Minx did not know, but it was already starting to bring about a fever. It didn't matter. She had to rendezvous with Junebug and the others. Minx ran for it. The rumble from the explosion caused by the thermite grenades she'd planted echoed throughout the ziggurat.

Swarm after swarm of Security Drones ran past the location where 808, Professor Proxy, and Floppy were hiding. 808 looked down at his Grimoire. There was a confirmation message on the map.

Security Nodes Deactivated...

Security Shield Offline...

The Hive placed the entire ziggurat on high alert. Our heroes waited for the last swarm to clear out in the direction of the last explosion. When all seemed safe, 808 ran out first, then Floppy, then Professor Proxy. When they entered the Occult Bureau's central command center, there were several Engineering Drones seated at the Hive's central mainframe supercomputer monitoring the reactor levels. 808 pulled out the MK Ultra Mark I & II and blew them all away. While the Engineering Drones smoldered, 808 took out his Grimoire and attached his Stream Ripper to the central mainframe supercomputer. He started ripping everything off of it that he could. The console's files flashed across the screen of the Grimoire. 808 took out a Thunderclap EMP and handed it to Professor Proxy. 808 grabbed the other Thunderclap and ran to the other side of the reactor to plant it himself.

"You done on your side?" said Professor Proxy as he finished setting the Thunderclap's timer.

808 shook his head no. Without warning, Killer pounced on him. 808 was knocked flat on his back. He rolled around on the ground with Killer on top of him in an attempt to shake him loose. Killer's jaws and razor-sharp teeth snapped at 808's face over and over again.

Professor Proxy grabbed a Circuit Breaker off of one of the smoldering Engineering Drones, powered it up, and with everything he had swung it at Killer. He landed the Circuit Breaker with perfect precision right upside Killer's head.

"*Rarrrrrtt!*" whined Killer. He rolled across the floor. When Killer stopped rolling, he crawled back to his feet. Killer shook his head, and in the angriest of demonic faces, looked in the direction of 808 and Professor Proxy. He started to growl, *"Grrrrr!"*

Floppy pounced in front of 808 and Professor Proxy.

"Rrrrr!" Floppy growled back.

Killer attacked Floppy. Floppy counter-attacked with a bite to the back of Killer's neck. Killer rolled over a few times. Floppy let go. Killer's powerful jaws closed in and crunched right through Floppy's exterior armor, exposing the circuitry underneath. Floppy winced in pain and went for Killer's throat. With all the strength he could muster, Floppy ripped out Killer's throat. Killer went limp. Floppy tossed him like a broken toy into the abyss of the ziggurat's ventilation system.

808 ran back over to his Thunderclap and set its timer. The countdown began. 808 jumped up and ran over to the central mainframe supercomputer to unplug his Stream Ripper.

"Before you disconnect your Grimoire," said Professor Proxy, "we should use the Hive to send out a warning message to the people."

808 nodded his head in agreement and activated the video camera on his Grimoire. Professor Proxy recorded a brief message. 808 spliced it together with the video from the Podcaster of Officer Whistle Britches showing Viirus and Special Agent Scarzensky together before the assassination of Governor Champagne, the video of Viirus killing himself at the Crystal Ball from his visor, and the videos he'd ripped from the mainframe in the lab of Dr. Necropolis. 808 entered the command prompt on the screen of the monitor on the central mainframe supercomputer. He uploaded the video and started streaming the warning message over the Hive's Emergency Broadcast System. 808 unplugged his Stream Ripper. Together with Professor Proxy and Floppy, they stepped out from inside the central command center, with the hope in all of their hearts, that they'd just saved the people trapped in Zohar.

Meanwhile, just outside the southern zone, Junebug was running for his life with Sassy flying in front of him. He felt sick, and his lungs were burning. They passed a sign on the wall of the ziggurat indicating that they were approaching Hangar 18's southern entrance. Junebug stopped to catch his breath. Sassy fluttered in the air in front of him and shot a beam of light out of each of her eyes. A holographic projection of Professor Proxy appeared in front of Junebug.

"The Thunderclaps are armed," said Professor Proxy. *"Where is Minx and Officer Whistle Britches?"*

Junebug didn't know.

"We split up," he said with a hint of worry in his voice.

"Meet us at—"

Professor Proxy's transmission started to break up. It appeared to be an amplification spike. There was the sound of an audio stream turned into a low-bit-rate static mixed with the garbled-up echo of Sassy's voice box. She squawked and shook her head like she had a headache. Something was hurting her. The thought crossed Junebug's mind that the Occult Bureau might be trying to intercept any form of communication between their group and silence it.

"Professor we can't make out what you're saying," said Junebug.

The signal died.

"The transmission just cut-out," said Professor Proxy to 808. He was none the wiser that in the selfsame moment in time that his transmission cut out, Sassy was blown up against the wall leading to Hangar 18's southern entrance. She was still alive, but the blast had rattled her, nonetheless. Junebug's stomach dropped when he looked in the direction of the blast. It was a death squad of mercenaries, and they had Lieutenant Blood, Specialist Gutts, and Corporal Gore with them.

31

GRAVITY BOOTS

Chaos filled every corner of the city of Zohar when the Hive's Emergency Broadcast System interrupted WXTZ Channel 13. The inhabitants of Zohar looked on in amazement. Their amazement turned to anger when they realized just how awful the lies of Johnny Lyes were. They now knew that the IPTV networks could not be trusted, that the operations of Controlled Substances Incorporated were diabolical, and that the Supreme Council had plotted their obliteration. The video recording of Professor Proxy's warning streamed in every home and business. It echoed throughout every street and streamed on anything with a screen no matter how large, or small. Every billboard, smartphone, and tablet carried the dire warning of Professor Proxy.

"People of Zohar, your lives are in danger. Nekron contains Nekrobytes. If you take this nekrobiotic, you will die. Do not comply with Supreme Council Resolution 33."

From one end of Zohar to the other, the inhabitants of the city rioted. They resisted the mercenaries in the Imperial Armada and destroyed the Occult Bureau's drones that were with them as they went door to door in a futile attempt to force the inhabitants of the city to take the nekrobiotic created by Controlled Substances Incorporated. Johnny Lyes ran for his life when Zohar's concerned citizens ransacked the studios of WXTZ Channel. He didn't make it very far before an angry viewer with a sawed-off shotgun blew him in half, and a WXTZ Channel 13 news van was set ablaze with Lolita Sanchez trapped inside.

Back inside the ziggurat, Officer Whistle Britches had been running for what seemed forever when his communicator started to vibrate. He pulled it out of his pocket and looked at the screen. It was Professor Proxy.

"Whistle Britches, where are you?" he said.

The body of Killer flew by Officer Whistle Britches at a lightning fast speed.

"Inside the ziggurat's ventilation system," said Officer Whistle Britches. He looked up to make sure that nothing else was falling in his direction.

"I think Junebug's in trouble," said Professor Proxy. *"Our transmission was interrupted. I can't reach him."*

"I lost my link with him, too," said Officer Whistle Britches. "His last coordinates showed that he was close to Hangar 18."

808 searched his Grimoire for any information on Hangar 18 that he might have ripped from the Hive's central mainframe supercomputer. The coordinates of Hangar 18 appeared on its screen. 808 tugged at Professor Proxy's lab coat and handed him the Grimoire.

"808's Grimoire is showing that Hangar 18 is an aerial loading dock," said Professor Proxy.

"Yeah, I know where it's at," said Officer Whistle Britches. *"That's where the Star Gazer refuels."*

"We'll meet you there," said Professor Proxy.

"I'm on my way," said Officer Whistle Britches.

A few paces west of Hangar 18's southern entrance, Junebug ran for his life. Sassy flew as fast as she could in front of him. Lasers whizzed past them. Lieutenant Blood, Specialist Gutts, and Corporal Gore chased Junebug for so long in the corridor outside of Hangar 18 that eventually they came to Hangar 18's western entrance. Junebug ran inside. A swarm of Security Drones were waiting. Junebug shucked a grenade from the Behemoth into the middle of the swarm. The grenade exploded. Junebug and Sassy dove for cover. Pieces of drones flew in every direction.

In the ventilation system, Officer Whistle Britches could hear and feel the explosion. It almost shook both of his Gravity Boots loose. One foot disconnected. Officer Whistle Britches dangled for a moment and locked it back in place. He continued running in the direction of the explosion. When Officer Whistle Britches arrived at Hangar 18, he peered through an air vent that overlooked the battle. It was pure carnage. The mechanical remains of destroyed drones lay everywhere. The few Security Drones not destroyed in the explosion had Junebug pinned down. Lieutenant Blood commanded several Tactical Drones to begin encircling him. Officer Whistle Britches opened up a communications link with Professor Proxy. It connected. Professor Proxy appeared on the screen of his communicator.

"I'm at Hangar 18," said Officer Whistle Britches. "Junebug's below me with Sassy. A swarm of drones and a death squad of mercenaries have got them pinned down. I don't know how much longer they can hold out."

"We heard the explosion," said Professor Proxy. "We're by the eastern entrance."

Officer Whistle Britches glanced over the rows of unloaded containers and saw Professor Proxy, 808, and Floppy hid amongst them.

"I can see you," he said.

"Good, we're going to need you to use the DDT if we're going to get out of here alive," said Professor Proxy.

Officer Whistle Britches kicked out the air vent and popped his head out the other side and screamed, "Cover me!"

Professor Proxy looked at 808. He had the MK Ultra Mark I & II locked and loaded. Behind his head, a hazardous materials label on the side of a disassembled aerial dispersal unit caught the eye of Professor Proxy. It was next to some empty barrels of Nekrotek. That's when it hit Professor Proxy. The Star Gazer was going to spray Nekrotek throughout the city. It didn't matter if you wanted to take Nekron or not. The Star Gazer was going to blanket the city in a nekrotik gas no one would be able to escape. His stomach sank, and his thoughts were interrupted by the sound of Officer Whistle Britches hitting the launch pad of Hangar 18 like a shooting star. The bottoms of Officer Whistle Britches feet stung like they were on fire. He powered up the DDT and sent a blast of quantum energy rippling through Hangar 18, that destroyed everything in its path.

Meanwhile, not too far away from our heroes current location, Minx stumbled into an armory with an open wound that continued to fester and fever. In front of her were several crates of medical supplies used by mercenaries when they were out on patrol. Minx opened one and took out a Trilock, a multipurpose medical device used for sewing up wounds. She took out a packet of FusionGel, a nanite repair paste, and cleaned the wound. Once there was no longer any pus present, Minx clamped down on both sides of her separated flesh with the Trilock.

"Agggh!" she screamed.

The Trilock brought her wounded flesh back together again, and the FusionGel numbed the pain. Once the wound was sealed, Minx grabbed a couple of thermite grenades and a Tetsuo 2600 machine gun off the top of a crate. Minx exited the armory and ran in the direction of all the gunfire and explosions she kept hearing as fast as she could. Minx took out her communicator. Her link with Junebug was dead. Minx's thoughts of Junebug turned to worry. She opened up a communications link with Professor Proxy.

Still hidden amongst the unloaded containers and empty barrels of Nekrotek, Minx appeared on Professor Proxy's communicator. It was obvious she was hurt.

"Minx are you alright?" said Professor Proxy.

"*I'm fine,*" said Minx. "*Is Junebug with you? I lost my communications link with him.*"

"We've found him, but so has a death squad of mercenaries," said Professor Proxy. "As far as the communications link, the Occult Bureau is jamming it somehow. We're communicating through a separate frequency on Floppy's packet-sniffer that they haven't become aware of yet."

"*I'm on my way,*" said Minx.

"Be careful," said Professor Proxy. The transmission ended. Behind him, from an ammo crate unloaded from an Imperial Weapons Transport, Professor Proxy grabbed a Scattershot, a multi-barrel, particle accelerating, hand-held, plasma cannon. 808 stuck his head out from behind the barrels of Nekrotek. Junebug was sweating bullets.

Every time he tried to stick his head up and fire the Behemoth, a drone shot him back down.

"I hope Minx is alright," Junebug said to Sassy.

Professor Proxy synced the targeting system of the Scattershot to Floppy's optics.

"We've only got one shot at this," he said.

Floppy nodded that he understood and took off running across the loading dock. It was child's play. Professor Proxy came out from behind the barrels of Nekrotek, Scattershot in hand, and laid waste to every drone Floppy locked-on to with his optics. 808 opened fire with the MK Ultra Mark I & II. The few seconds that their sudden attack provided Junebug with enabled him to come up from behind the shipping containers he was trapped behind. He made a break for it across Hangar 18 to a safer position. Junebug's balls took Lieutenant Blood, Specialist Gutts, and Corporal Gore by surprise, and angered them all to no end.

When Minx entered Hangar 18, she aimed the Tetsuo 2600 and pulled its trigger. Drones began to drop to the ground like dead flies. The tide had turned, and everyone knew it.

Lieutenant Blood, Specialist Gutts, Corporal Gore, and the mercenaries in their death squad provided cover fire for Dr. Necropolis. A Medical Drone loaded Torment inside the Star Gazer. A dozen Psyborgs opened fire on our heroes. Junebug and Minx fired back. Security Drones dropped to the ground one by one. Dr. Necropolis and the Psyborgs guarding him entered the Star Gazer and prepared to take off.

Professor Proxy looked at 808 and said, "We've got to stop the Star Gazer from taking off. They're going to use the Nekrotek inside of it to mutate everyone in the city."

808 nodded to Professor Proxy that he understood and ran across the launch pad with Sassy fluttering in the air behind him.

"808, wait!" shouted Professor Proxy, but it was too late. 808 jumped up and caught the edge of the cargo bay door of the Star Gazer. He hoisted himself over the edge and rolled inside just in time to stop the door from closing. Sassy fluttered in behind him.

Officer Whistle Britches aimed the DDT at the Star Gazer. Junebug knew that was the wrong thing to do. He lunged at Officer Whistle Britches in an attempt to try to stop him.

"Don't shoot!" screamed Junebug.

It was too late.

Junebug tackled Officer Whistle Britches the moment pulled the trigger. The blast from the DDT missed the Star Gazer and hit a bunch of unloaded barrels of Nekrotek stacked together in a pile. The explosion was so massive it partially engulfed the Star Gazer as it lifted off the launch pad and made its way out of the ziggurat and into the night sky. Lieutenant Blood, Specialist Gutts, Corporal Gore, and the mercenaries in their death squad were swallowed up by the explosion. Their bubbling flesh burned their bones to a blackened crisp.

"Ahhh!" they screamed in agony.

Officer Whistle Britches was horrified by what he saw. Junebug grabbed him by the arm.

"We've got to get out of here!" he shouted.

32

STAR GAZER

Inside the Star Gazer, 808's brain zaps were getting worse. His cybernetic muscles and his mind were beginning to glitch out from time to time. 808 shook his head and slapped the side of his helmet with the palm of his armored hand where Mistress LaReaux shot him. His optics came back into focus. 808 had to concentrate hard. Otherwise, his vision became impaired. The first thing that he saw was HazMat Drones loading rows of stacked barrels of Nekrotek into the aerial dispersal units that would spray the mutagenic gas across the city. There was enough inside the hull of the ship to turn everyone in Zohar into a mindless raving mutant.

Sassy flew up and perched herself on a rafter. She sent out a three-dimensional pulse signal that mapped the interior of the Star Gazer and synced it with the internal heads-up display on 808's visor. Dr. Necropolis was alerted to 808's presence by a Security Drone. He activated Torment. The evil creature's eyes filled with a demonic glow. Dr. Necropolis ordered Torment and the Psyborgs guarding him to hunt 808 down. Sassy scanned the cargo hold and locked-on to the Psyborgs as targets. There were too many of them for her to attack at one time, stealth was to be the key to their survival. Sassy alerted 808 to the location of each Psyborg so that he could avoid detection and not get ambushed into another gunfight like they'd experienced inside the ziggurat. 808 placed some Snot Box remote-controlled proximity mines on the rows of stacked barrels of Nekrotek around him. It was a foolish thing to do because if a Psyborg or one of the HazMat Drones walked by one of the Snot Boxes, it would explode. The explosion would ignite the Nekrotek and kill him right along with any Psyborgs and HazMat Drones in the area but it was a chance 808 was willing to take to save his mother and the people he loved. Professor Proxy, Junebug, Minx, Officer Whistle Britches, and Floppy, they were his friends, his family, he'd already faced death once and was ready to die for them if that's what it took.

808 came to the end of one of the vast rows of Nekrotek. He found himself in front of several unloaded aerial dispersal units used to turn liquid Nekrotek into an aerosol spray. The readout on 808's Grimoire provided by Sassy showed that Dr. Necropolis was running the Star Gazer with little more than a skeleton crew.

In front of each aerial dispersal unit was a workstation that a HazMat Drone would use to control the dispersion of Nekrotek. 808 knew he had to shut them all down if he was going to save the city. A head-to-head fight with the HazMat Drones loading Nekrotek into the aerial dispersal units was out of the question. He'd have to hack the workstation to shut the aerial dispersal units down.

808 approached the workstation nearest to him and attached his Stream Ripper to an open data port.

Reset...

Glitch...

Hack...

808 cracked the workstation's manual override command sequence and gave the order for the aerial dispersal units to begin to shutdown.

Shutdown Sequence Initiated...

Professor Proxy appeared on the internal heads-up display on 808's visor. He was using Floppy's packet sniffer to stream a signal to him. A few distorted words tried to come through. Professor Proxy's image scrambled. The signal from Floppy's packet sniffer degraded more and more the further the Star Gazer flew away from the ziggurat.

A reflection appeared on the screen of the monitor on the workstation in front of 808. He ducked just in time to miss a punch thrown by Torment. His fist shattered the screen of the monitor. There was a small explosion. All the Psyborgs in the Star Gazer heard it. They converged on 808's location. He ran and hid behind some barrels of Nekrotek. Torment walked between the rows looking for 808. He stopped close to the spot where 808 was hidden and sniffed the air. Torment knew 808 was around there, but he wasn't sure where. Torment's shadow ran up several stacked barrels of Nekrotek. He walked over to the next isle readied for dispersal.

Once Torment was out of sight, 808 got up and tippy-toed in the opposite direction. He looked over his shoulder and did not pay attention to what was in front of him. 808 stumbled into a toolbox left behind by the Star Gazer's maintenance crew. The toolbox fell to the floor and made a loud bang heard over all the noise made by the aerial dispersal units. Torment turned around and scanned the area. He saw 808 running for his life and chased after him. Psyborgs opened fire with endocrine disrupting rounds because they wouldn't ignite the Nekrotek. 808 turned and opened fire on Torment with the MK Ultra Mark I & II. Round after round hit Torment and penetrated his tough, sewn together hide. He kept running faster and faster in 808's direction no matter how many times 808 shot him. Torment swung at 808. 808 ducked. The punch missed him and collided with a row of barrels of Nekrotek stacked on top of one another.

The stack of Nekrotek crumbled, barrel after barrel fell on top of Torment. 808 dove for cover. Squealing like a disemboweled pig hanging from a hook, Torment struggled to get up. The more he tried, the deeper he was crushed under the sheer weight of all the Nekrotek piled on top of him. One row over, on the other side of the pile, stood a Psyborg. The Psyborg opened fire on 808 and approached one of the Snot Boxes. 808 knew all hell was about to break loose. On the floor around him, Nekrotek was pouring out of the ruptured barrels that had fallen onto Torment. 808 ran away from the pile as fast as he could.

The Psyborg crossed the threshold.

The Snot Box exploded.

The pile of leaking Nekrotek ignited and exploded. The explosion ripped a massive hole in the hull of the Star Gazer. HazMat Drones, Psyborgs, and anything close to the opening not secured to the floor of the Star Gazer flew out of the smoking hole.

Nekrotek spewed everywhere.

Sassy flapped her wings and squawked as loud as she could as she hovered above a Battle Box secured to the floor of the Star Gazer. 808 opened the Battle Box. Inside was a Nosferatu jetpack. 808 attached it to his body armor. Sassy transformed and latched onto it. Their hardware synced. Sassy's aerial display merged with the internal heads-up display on 808's visor. 808 walked over to the blown out section of the Star Gazers hull and peered out into the open sky above the city. What he saw could only be described as apocalyptic. The riots had taken their toll. Zohar was on the verge of complete collapse. Nekrobytes swarmed the populace. The sky above the Temple of Oblivion looked eldritch as it swirled like a whirlpool. The Gateway to the Void and the Sigil of the Great Architect of the Universe were coming into alignment. Sassy knew what 808 was thinking. She squawked. He jumped.

The Star Gazer exploded.

The Nosferatu expelled a blast of kinetic energy. 808 and Sassy raced through the sky.

In the Torture Garden, Professor Proxy, Officer Whistle Britches, Junebug, Minx, and Floppy ran for their lives. They were almost to the steps that lead up to the Temple of Oblivion. Swarms of Security Drones chased after them.

Minx tossed a thermite grenade. It rolled across the ground of Torture Garden and exploded in the middle of one of the swarms. Mangled parts flew everywhere. The Security Drones that survived the explosion continued to open fire on our heroes with their Baphomets. The Occult Bureau sent everything it had at them.

Professor Proxy returned fire with the Scattershot.

"This is not going to end well!" screamed Officer Whistle Britches as he opened fire with the DDT.

"All we need to do is hold out for a few more minutes!" shouted Professor Proxy. "The Thunderclaps are about to blow!"

33

INTO OBLIVION

The naked body of Princess Destiny looked lifeless as it lay on the Altar of the Sleeping Virgin when Mystre entered the Temple of Oblivion into the dreamlike geometry of the Jewel of Wisdom. He held the Codex Magicka in one hand and the Staff of the Illuminati in the other. Alexis and Xavier were behind him, followed by the Disciples of Oblivion carrying the sarcophagus of their master.

"Why is she still alive?" shouted Councilman Soros. In extreme anger, he rose up from his seat next to the dais the Throne of Oblivion sat atop. Behind him, the centurions in the Order of the Trapezoid protecting the Supreme Council stepped forward and beheaded each member of the council with their Widowmakers, one by one, all but Councilman Soros. He was stomped and beaten to a bloody pulp. Two centurions seized him by both arms and drug his half-dead body across the temple. Councilman Soros left a trail of blood on the floor behind him before being dropped at the feet of Xavier.

"Did you really think that I would kill her to please you?" he said.

The Disciples of Oblivion opened the sarcophagus and placed the bones of Oblivion in the center of the Triangle of Manifestation at the center of the Sigil of the Great Architect of the Universe. Mystre and the Disciples of Oblivion turned and exited the temple.

"I-I, will k-k-kill, you f-f-for, t-t-his," stuttered Councilman Soros. The old bastard remained unbroken.

Xavier could see the look of horror written all over the face of Alexis.

"What would you have me do?" he said. "Show him the same mercy he showed your father? Earlier this evening this crusty old turd dared to joke about turning you into one of the temple prostitutes in front of me? If it were up to him, you would be chained to one of the Pillars of Eternity, to be raped by whatever loathsome and diseased creature decided to crawl between your legs. Your death moans would be filled with vulgar lusts. Even as you drew your last breath, you would find no peace for there is always some lesser beast of the field willing to have sex with a corpse, if for no other reason than it simply needs a place to cum. Now I ask you, does the impotent bottom-feeder who would cast you down amongst such filth deserve your mercy?"

"Y-yo-you, sh-sha-shall, pay, fuh-for th-this m-my young Thorn. You shall pay," stuttered Councilman Soros with all the strength he could muster.

Xavier remained unshaken by the threats of Councilman Soros as he gripped the hilt of the Midnight Sun and removed it from the sword pedestal next to the Throne of Oblivion.

"The undoing of the Great Work of the Great Architect of the Universe is at hand," he said. "Do you know what that means you old fool? No, of course, you don't. It is beyond your feeble-minded comprehension to understand even the simplest lessons of creation. The undoing of the Great Work of the Great Architect of the Universe is the restoration of the natural order of all things. Harmony, equilibrium, it is the act of putting back in its proper place that which should never have strayed from the path of Oblivion. You fancy yourself like all the other useless eaters on the Supreme Council, a chosen people, exalted and favored by Oblivion above all others. But in truth, thou art the most profane of all misguided things."

Xavier walked to the center of the Sigil of the Great Architect of the Universe. He plucked the Jewel of Wisdom out of the air and placed it into the pommel of the Midnight Sun.

"I-I, will ha-h-have m-my, revenge!" said Councilman Soros.

A Medical Drone presented Xavier with a syringe full of

nekrobiotic hatchlings. Xavier motioned with his hand in the direction of Councilman Soros. The Medical Drone grabbed him by the hair, pulled his head back, and injected the contents of the syringe into his neck. When they entered Councilman Soros' circulatory system, the nekrobiotic hatchlings went straight to his spleen and hatched, beginning the process of mutating him into a Goyum, just like the grotesques Alexis had seen in the lab of Dr. Necropolis.

"Thou art my perfect ashlar, councilman," said Xavier. "The cornerstone from which we shall begin to build a new world."

Xavier kicked Councilman Soros' mutated body like a stray dog. In fear, it scurried across the floor and out of the temple. Alexis was aghast at what she was seeing.

"Xavier, this has to stop!" she said. "How can you stand there and participate in the creation of such a thing?"

"Do you know the price I paid to Mystre for your life?" said Xavier. "Did you think his kindness was free, that it did not come without a cost? I swore an unbreakable oath before the Priestess of Oblivion that upon my families once immortal soul and bloodline that I would help free her lover's spirit from the Void. For all eternity, he is my lord and master. His will is my will. She promised me that in return for my faithfulness, Oblivion would heal our child and that we would be spared his divine judgment when his wrath is poured out upon what remains of the Gardens of Eternity. That is the price I paid for the vial that would save your life, Alexis. That is how much I love you and our son."

Alexis couldn't believe what she'd just heard.

"Xavier, you've been deceived," she said. "You've allowed Mystre and Psydonia to fill your head with lies."

Xavier grinned.

"My vision has never been more clear, my thoughts soberer, my life more filled with purpose," he said. "Don't you see that all you need to do is take your place by my side and welcome the Spirit of Oblivion into your heart, as I have, and our son, our beloved family, will be restored to us? All we have to do is be obedient, to wipe the enemies of Oblivion from the face of what remains of the Gardens of Eternity, so that they can never cry out to the Great Architect of the Universe, again, and we can all be together forever."

"That is a lie, Xavier!" shouted Alexis. "If you destroy that sigil you will loose upon this world a demon that will enslave everyone in it, including you. Can't you see that or have you become that damn blind?"

The look crawling across Xavier's face spoke for itself. In his hurt, in his quest to regain the love of Alexis and undo all the pain and heartache caused by the mutilation of their son, he'd lost his way. The words coming forth from the mouth of Alexis had no meaning. In his mind, Xavier had done the right thing.

"Why can't you see that we have it in our power to begin anew?" said Xavier. "We can be immortal together, you and I? The Lord of the Void will deny us nothing. We will rise above the heavens and become like gods."

Alexis could take no more. The shadows throughout the darkness of the temple had begun to whisper and beckon to her as the moans of the temple prostitutes mixed with the chants and incantations of Mystre and the Disciples of Oblivion surrounding the naked body of Princess Destiny grew louder and louder outside. In a numbing grip of despair, she fought back the tears welling in her eyes.

"You're not a god, Xavier," said Alexis.

"No, my beloved, I'm not," said Xavier. In anger, he raised the Midnight Sun upward toward the heavens and the Void's dying light. The ethereal vibrations were getting stronger and stronger. A spatial shift opened up a rift in both space and time. A beam of demonic dimensional energy filled the blade of the Midnight Sun with a power only one other had ever known. Xavier plunged the Midnight Sun into the Sigil of the Great Architect of the Universe. Encircled by all the signs of the zodiac, the Spirit of Oblivion poured out of the Void and engulfed the temple.

"I am Oblivion!" screamed the possessed body of Xavier.

Alexis stumbled backward. She fell to the floor of the temple.

In the sky outside, 808 and Sassy raced toward the Temple of Oblivion attached to the Nosferatu. 808 opened fire on Mystre with the MK Ultra Mark I & II and shot the dagger he was about to plunge into the naked body of Princess Destiny from his hands. The Disciples of Oblivion and the temple prostitutes scattered in every direction. Mystre ran for cover inside the temple, knocking everything and everyone in his path to ground, including the disciple holding the Codex Magicka.

A dumb-founded centurion dropped his Widowmaker. Alexis made her move. She scrambled to her feet. Alexis grabbed the Widowmaker and hurled it at Oblivion with all the strength she could muster. Oblivion swung the Midnight Sun and knocked the spinning Widowmaker away before it could hit him. He let out a demonic scream and ran after Alexis with all the hatred that all of creation had ever known burning in his black heart.

808 and Sassy flew into the temple and opened fire on Oblivion. He screamed in anger and swung the Midnight Sun at them when they flew by. The attack missed. Seeing a moment of opportunity Alexis reached into her boot and threw one of her Ionic Daggers at Oblivion. It struck him in one of his eyes.

"Agghhh!" Oblivion screamed in pain. He dropped the Midnight Sun and clutched his face. The mutilated socket was throbbing in agonizing pain.

Alexis grabbed the Midnight Sun off the floor. She raised it over her head and in an arcing motion, buried the blade in the middle of the skull of Oblivion. Blood spewed everywhere. His other eyeball popped out, and he collapsed to the floor. The Spirit of Oblivion poured from the dying body of Xavier. Like the Four Winds of the Gardens of Eternity, it drifted off into the night and made its escape. Without a healthy body, the Spirit of Oblivion had no home, without the death of Princess Destiny as a blood sacrifice, the ritual was still incomplete.

"F-f-forgive me," said Xavier with a raspy tone in his voice that did everything it could to hold back his death rattle. The lies of Psydonia and Mystre haunted his mind.

Princess Destiny awoke. 808 and Sassy landed beside her. 808 stripped the dead body of a centurion of his imperial cloak and placed it around the naked body of Princess Destiny.

Xavier's trembling hand reached up to touch Alexis one last time to the sound of an evil woman's demonic laughter. With every dying breath, it grew louder and louder. The Temple of Oblivion turned as black as the night sky. The skin all over the body of Alexis began to crawl. Psydonia descended from the shadows atop the temple on a single red thread that looked like a laser. She had a magical staff, the

Orbweaver, in her hand. All around Alexis, in the darkness of the temple, she could see an almost endless array of glowing red eyes. The Araknidz that protected Psydonia were spawning.

"Thou art truly a fool," said Psydonia to Xavier. He took his last dying breath and passed away. Xavier's spirit was sent hurdling into the Void to replace Oblivion's. The Araknidz wrapped his carcass in a cocoon and carried it off into the darkness.

"You tricked him!" shouted Alexis.

"He deceived himself," said Psydonia. The mutilated flesh of her face was maggot eaten and filled with parasites. "Just like you chose to believe the feeble little lie that it was Councilman Soros that was responsible for exposing you to our Nekrobytes. It was I who told Mystre to use his puppet to expose you to them so that Xavier would have no choice but to accept our offer and do our bidding."

"You're a liar!" screamed Alexis.

"No my little one," said Psydonia, "the truth is a poison far more venomous than I."

The two Thunderclap EMPs placed on the tryptamine reactor at the center of the ziggurat exploded. A ring of fire rippled up level after level throughout the ziggurat destroying everything in its path.

Buh-doooom!

The Temple of Oblivion shook. Huge chunks of the temple's roof fell and crushed the Disciples of Oblivion as the floor underneath them became brittle and collapsed. Those not crushed in the chaos ran in every direction in a desperate attempt to escape with their lives. Mystre stepped into a hidden stairwell concealed within the shadows of the temple.

"Get out of here!" shouted Alexis.

808 picked the Codex Magicka up off the ground outside of the temple and handed it to Princess Destiny. He grabbed her around her waist. Sassy fired up the Nosferatu. A kinetic blast from its afterburners sent them flying away from the Altar of the Sleeping Virgin and out into the Torture Garden. They landed in front of Professor Proxy.

"Where is Alexis?" he said.

"She's still inside the temple," said Princess Destiny.

Back inside the Temple of Oblivion, with the Midnight Sun in hand,

Alexis freed Maximillion from his chains. He roared. A second explosion shook the temple. Alexis bound the Midnight Sun to the back of her armor and mounted Maximillion. Together they raced across the checkerboard tile floor of the temple. Psydonia fired her Orbweaver at Alexis. Maximillion leapt out of the Temple of Oblivion. The shot missed. A quantum explosion of epic proportions disintegrated everything around them.

"Bring me back that jewel!" screamed Psydonia to her Araknidz. The nightmarish horde chased after Alexis and Maximillion. Psydonia ran behind them. The staircase and the many pillars that led to the Temple of Oblivion crumbled around Alexis. Maximillion ran toward the ground below at a breakneck speed.

Professor Proxy, 808, Junebug, Minx, Sassy, Officer Whistle Britches, and Floppy armed their weapons. Maximillion reached the bottom of the staircase. One by one our heroes picked off the Araknidz. They seemed too numerous to count. Psydonia dove from the staircase and attacked Alexis. A blast from the Orbweaver rippled past Professor Proxy. Officer Whistle Britches fired the DDT at Psydonia.

Thooooooom!

Alexis, turned Maximillion as time slowly came to a stand-still, gripped the Midnight Sun as tightly as she could and leapt forward from her mount. The final and fatal blow chopped the human half of Psydonia from her robotic half. The upper body of Psydonia slid apart from the lower. Sparks of electricity shot out in every direction. A maddening scream disintegrated from her lips, "Noooooo!" The upper part of her severed body hit the ground face first. Psydonia's muffled scream died. Alexis kicked her over. There was no sign of life in Psydonia's eyes.

All seemed lost for the followers of Oblivion.

Out in the city, the mercenaries in the Imperial Armada ran for their lives from a people who'd had enough. There were no drones to protect them. Not a single Nekrobyte was operational.

Perched atop a tree limb in the Torture Garden, Sassy saw Mystre trying to slip away undetected from a secret passageway. She sent the visuals from her optics to Floppy's heads-up display. Floppy locked-on to Mystre. His attempt to run away would be both feeble and futile. Floppy ran after Mystre as fast as he could and tackled him.

"Ughnnf!" groaned Mystre when he hit the ground.

808, Officer Whistle Britches, Junebug, Minx, Professor Proxy, and Princess Destiny surrounded him. Alexis bent over and picked up a Baphomet off of one of the deactivated Enforcer Drones.

"It's over, Mystre," she said.

The face of Mystre remained solemn. He pointed his bony finger at Alexis.

"There are still a great many things about the wrath of Oblivion for you to learn, you miserable cunt," he said. "This is far from over."

Alexis raised the barrel of the Baphomet in her hand and pulled its trigger. The laser shot from the barrel of the Baphomet ripped through Mystre's skull and revealed that it wasn't Mystre that she'd shot at all, but a robotic decoy of the hierophant. To the amazement of everyone, the android buzzed and short-circuited in what seemed like a moment that would last forever, yet within its last cybernetic breath, the morbid climax to a long dark journey was now complete.

EPILOGUE

THE PALACE OF DESTINY

All over the Black Sun Empire, the descendants of the Flower Children celebrated our heroes victory as the inhabitants of Zohar gathered outside the Palace of Destiny. In the Fellowship Hall, Destiny announced that the ziggurat and what remained of the ruins of the Temple of Oblivion would be torn down. Alexis placed the Midnight Sun, the Jewel of Wisdom, and the Codex Magicka in the palace for safekeeping. The fanfare of our heroes victory parade was majestic. Together they were triumphant and loyal to one another unto the very end. Streamers and confetti rained down amongst dazzling laser light displays and the thunderous applause of a people that had been spared a fate worse than death. They were overjoyed. Cheering and gleeful smiles filled their faces with laughter and merry-making. Our heroes were awed by the adulation of the crowd. The noise and excitement around them was deafening. Our heroes were called forth so that Princess Destiny could shower them with the praise they deserved in accordance with the royal traditions of her family.

"Professor Proxy," said Princess Destiny, "it is you that I thank for finding a solution to the scourge that Dr. Necropolis has unleashed upon us all. There are many amongst our people that owe you their lives."

"Thank you, Your Majesty. It was my humble honor and duty," said

Professor Proxy. He accepted a medal, the Tears of Technology, it was the Black Sun Empire's highest scientific honor. Princess Destiny placed the medal around his neck. Professor Proxy deserved it, for he had created a Nekroblaster capable of molecular self-reassembly that enabled him to manufacture and distribute plenty of Halcyon 1138 even though the supply of available skull flowers was limited. Billions had died from nekrosis in the Golden Triangle, the refugee camps, and decaying Immortal Kingdoms before the destruction of the Hive, yet now there was hope. All were grateful for his accomplishments. This new invention saved their lives and that of their loved ones as well. Junebug was his first successful patient. Professor Proxy rose from his kneeling position and took his place next to Princess Destiny and Maximillion.

Officer Whistle Britches stepped forward and made his way up the steps that lead to Princess Destiny. He stumbled and almost fell. Everyone laughed and giggled, even Floppy snickered. Officer Whistle Britches regained his composure and tried to pretend as though nothing happened. He knelt down on one knee and bowed his head.

"Officer Whistle Britches, an excellent example of what it is our public servants should be, I present you with this," said Princess Destiny, "an imperial service medal for your valor. From this day forward, before all our people, you will be known as a Loyal Protector of the Black Sun Empire."

"Thank you, Your Majesty," said Officer Whistle Britches.

"I look forward to seeing you in my new Imperial Honor Guard," said Princess Destiny.

Floppy was also given a medal for his dog collar.

"*Rarf!*" he barked.

Officer Whistle Britches made his way to the side of Professor Proxy. Floppy sat down in front of him. Junebug and Minx walked up the steps of the Fellowship Hall beside each other. When they reached the last step, they knelt on one knee with their heads bowed.

"Junebug and Minx, I present the two of you with these imperial pardons for all your acts of piracy committed in the Port of Zohar and throughout the Black Sun Empire," said Princess Destiny. She presented Junebug and Minx with two small ornate boxes engraved with the Royal Seal of the Palace of Destiny on the outside. They opened them and saw two diamond necklaces, one in each box. Attached to each necklace was a pendant engraved with the declaration of their imperial pardons.

"Thank you, Your Majesty," said Junebug and Minx in unison.

Sassy squawked in approval. She fluttered toward Princess Destiny and landed before her with her head bowed. Sassy was given a miniature diamond necklace with a pendant attached to it too that was engraved with an imperial declaration that she was an imperial asset to Princess Destiny and under no circumstances was she ever to be damaged or encounter any harm. She kissed Princess Destiny on the hand and fluttered off. Sassy landed on the shoulder of Junebug.

808 walked up the steps of the Fellowship Hall. Alexis was behind him. At the last step, 808 took a knee and bowed his head.

"808," said Princess Destiny, "I present you these gold chains commemorating your imperil citizenship and rights of inheritance." Princess Destiny placed two gold chains around the neck of 808. He liked the look of all the gold around his neck. Attached to one chain was a pendant engraved with an imperial declaration granting him imperial citizenship and to the other chain a pendant engraved with an imperial declaration granting him the same imperial rights of inheritance that a child would expect to inherit from his parents and extended family. 808 threw up the Sign of the Horns as a thank you. Alexis smiled. The black velvet dress she had on was beautiful. Alexis took a knee with her head bowed. "And last but certainly not least, to you my dear sweet Alexis, with a gracious thank you in the name of all those that live and breathe in what remains of the Gardens of Eternity, I present you with this royal title."

Alexis opened a small ornate box engraved with the Royal Seal of the Palace of Destiny similar to the ones given to Junebug and Minx. Inside was a royal title to all of her family's noble lands. On these lands were the vineyards upon whom the citizens of the empire depended for a never-ending supply of Zoharian wine and champagne that had made her family a fortune for centuries.

"Thank you, Your Majesty," said Alexis.

"I also present you with this," said Princess Destiny. One of her servants stepped forth with a velvet pillow upon which sat something so beautiful words could not describe it. "An amulet, containing the

Eye of Oblivion, so that with the aid of the Codex Magicka you may
learn the secrets of the ancient electronic arts."

Once the awards ceremony ended, Princess Destiny and Alexis
stepped out into the courtyard behind the Fellowship Hall where
ornate sculptures were in abundance that told the story of those who
had walked the gardens of the royal palace over the countless centuries
long before it became Princess Destiny's. They were the symbols of a
stable tradition that led to some vineyards planted by the
Champagne's. Alexis came to the final resting place of both her mother
and father. The clouds in the sky cast a shadow that raced across the
ground and over both of their graves. Etched on her father's tomb was
the phrase, THERE IS NO DEATH FOR THE HONORABLE. Perhaps
in the next life, Alexis thought to herself, she would be reunited with
them. A sorrowful grief came upon her. Her spirit was stricken with
despair. Alexis inhaled and exhaled in what seemed like a moment
that swallowed up both space and time, for it was in that single breath
of life that her own mortality began to haunt her. The years she had
now seen seemed so few and the ones that she had left, so easily
numbered.

Princess Destiny recognized her pain. She too had lost both her
parents when she was very young. It was a fraternity that every living
thing that walked upon what remained of the Gardens of Eternity
would become part of sooner or later, both the rich and the poor, the
ignorant and the learned, the young and the old, both man and beast,
our graves are waiting for us all beneath the ground where the skull
flowers grow.

"I miss them," said Alexis to Princess Destiny.

"You will always miss them," said Princess Destiny. "Do not allow
yourself to be filled with sorrow or your mind to be filled with the lies
of the Spirit of Oblivion, for if you do, you will one day find yourself in
a time and place doing as Xavier did."

"Will it never end?" said Alexis.

"Not until the hearts of men and women are no longer tempted by
the Spirit of Oblivion, until that day, we are all cursed to forever
struggle to allude its demonic grasp," said Princess Destiny.

"I could have done more. I should have done more. Father always
said I should quit kidding around and be more responsible, that I

should do right by my people and my family name. I wasn't there to protect him," said Alexis. She placed her hand on the statue of Governor Champagne.

"Regret will plague your mind," said Princess Destiny. "Don't give in to those thoughts. Honor your loved ones daily in your prayers and in every breath of what life you have left."

"They are together now," said Alexis. "I know that they're happy."

"Indeed, they are," said Princess Destiny before steering the conversation into another topic of discussion. "I have been reading your latest research into cybernetic biology."

Alexis became nervous.

"Did you find it interesting?" she said.

"I know that 808 is your son," said Princess Destiny.

"Who told you?" said Alexis.

"It was your father who first told me that it was the Nekrobytes that caused your miscarriage, but it was Professor Proxy who slipped up and revealed that there was more to 808 than meets the eye," said Princess Destiny. "Why did you not tell me that you did not lose your child? Did you not trust me?"

Alexis was silent for a moment.

"I was scared that if the Supreme Council found out what we'd done, they'd hunt 808 down and have him destroyed," she said. "So I kept it a secret from everyone."

"You should have come to me so that I could have helped you," said Princess Destiny. "My mother hid the secret truth of your family that you were all followers of the Great Architect of the Universe from not only the outside world but my own father because she loved your family that much. You are the closest thing I've ever had to a sister. You know that don't you?"

"I know that now," said Alexis.

"Never allow your thoughts to become so clouded as to think that you can't come to me and confide in all things no matter how troubling," said Princess Destiny.

"I won't," said Alexis. "I promise."

"With that out of the way, might I inquire as to what you have planned for the future?" said Princess Destiny.

"I don't know," said Alexis.

"If I may be so bold as to make a suggestion?" said Princess Destiny.

"You may," said Alexis.

"For now, the militia will protect the city," said Princess Destiny. "But they have no leader. I want you to be that guiding light."

"You want me to lead the militia?" said Alexis.

"If you're willing to accept the post, I will appoint you Supreme Commander of the Imperial Forces of the Black Sun Empire so that you can rebuild the Imperial Armada as you see fit," said Princess Destiny. "I know that under your protection, the Jewel of Wisdom will always be safe from the unholy spirit that now haunts our world."

"I don't know," said Alexis. "Surely, there is someone more capable than me?"

Princess Destiny saw the look of apprehension on the face of Alexis.

"We need you," she said with an inviting smile. "I need you."

Alexis thought for a moment. It was time for her to fulfill her duty to the royal family and her people like her father had always dreamed she would and to do right by the memory of her mother.

"Then I shall be here for you, for our people and for what remains of the Gardens of Eternity," said Alexis. And so it was that the two of them smiled and walked through the vineyards together, hand in hand, discussing what it was they could do to thwart the inevitable onslaught that one day soon would come from Mystre and the Spirit of Oblivion. There were many would-be disciples in the darkest corners and spider-haunted shadows of Zohar that secretly whispered that they would one day rebuild their master's temple and murder those who had a hand in its destruction, where the stars will shine forever, where the sky it never ends, where all will ride eternal, and the moonlight shall attend, but that is another story, amongst the riots and make-believe...